FALLEN

A novel by K.L. Silver

Copyright © 2016 K.L. Silver

ISBN: 978-1-928121-22-0

Dedication

To Empaths everywhere. I feel your joy and your pain.

Acknowledgments

Where to begin. I couldn't have done this without the support of my family.

Thank you.

But, family doesn't just mean the folks you're related to. Peter Domineck backs me every inch of the way.

Thank you.

Nancy Pracht has been by my side almost from day one. A fabulous PA and friend, she's a great help not only in holding the fort down while I'm in the 'Dungeon', writing, but as a sounding board, as well.

Thank you.

Michael Halliday is a great friend and fan. Everyone needs a cheerleader when you're down and not feeling up to the task. Michael puts the wind back in my sails.

Thank you.

Elise Sodeman is an amazing woman, period. As a Beta reader? Even better. She gets full credit for turning FALLEN from a cliffhanger – to a – well, you'll see.

Thank you

Alexandra Lucas does amazing work with covers, amongst other things. She's done all of mine so far and I can only hope she's on board to do them in the future.

Thank you.

The beautiful photo at the center is courtesy of TheJaan on Flicker.

Thank you.

Last but far from least, I have a Street Team that never ceases to blow me away. Their support, their various skills, their generosity of time of energy is a beautiful thing to behold. Special shout outs to Barbie, Mandi, Kimberly and Jamie.

Thank you.

I'm honored to have you all in my life.

Table of Contents

Chapter 1

With a long overdue click, Zoey closed the cyber-ledger. Her eyes burned and her low back ached. Not surprising after ten hours in 'the chair'.

Another ten hours...

She'd just paid some of the best gymnastics coaches, dance choreographers and ballet instructors on the planet – not to mention sports doctors, physical therapists, psychologists and nutritionists. New equipment was ordered to replace the old and the broken. Flights to upcoming competitions were booked. Her own meager paycheck was resting comfortably in her savings account.

Moaning through an exaggerated stretch, she smiled when the ancient office chair moaned right along with her. Rumor had it that at one time—way back when—the pathetic excuse for a chair had boasted an actual layer of padding between the threadbare upholstery and the solid cardboard base. She knew someone who knew someone who'd seen it with their own eyes.

She'd first set eyes on it as a spindly fourteen year old. Back then, it was molded to the ample behind of 'Mama' Peggy, wife of Jock and mother of six. Hailing from Hoxie, Kansas, population 1,081, Peggy's laughter came straight from her expansive belly. Her larger-than-life personality fit her larger-than life frame to a T. With a grin as wide as her behind and more infectious than measles, she'd caught Zoey's scrawny wrist in her pudgy hand. With a tug, she'd reeled her in like a yo-yo at the end of its string and hugged her to her bosom in welcome.

It'd been her first day at the gym and she'd really, *really* needed a hug. It was at that moment that Peggy became her surrogate mother. She called her for advice to this day.

Reaching for her water bottle, Zoey still didn't get up. Even now, she was in no hurry to leave. With her roommate out with the love-of-her-life-du-jour, home meant a cold sandwich and another overseas phone call to her biological mother, who still hadn't returned the last one. In avoidance mode, Zoey flipped the cap, guzzled down some H2O, and flexed her numbed butt-cheeks. The chair creaked in protest, seemingly offended by her nervy attempt to seek comfort. When some feeling returned to her flattened gluteals, she leaned back. Tucking her long legs beneath her, she exhaled a sigh of relief.

Not that long ago, The National Gymnastics Training Center was hovering on the brink of bankruptcy – its founder dead of a massive stroke. The NGTC was Hal Edward's dream, his baby, and his one true passion in life. Anyone who doubted that need only ask one of his menage of frustrated ex-wives. Like Groundhog Day, the scenario never varied. One after another, they came and they left—fed up to *here* with playing second fiddle to a sport.

Even at the age of seventy-three, Hal had shown no sign of slowing down. Strong like a bull and twice as stubborn, he'd tended to the gym's every detail—be it a problem with a girl's beam routine or a drippy faucet. Nothing was off limits. Nothing was too minute. Built from the ground up, it was Hal's domain, and he ruled it unchallenged.

Seeing that he was chosen as the National Women's Team coach not once, not twice—but *three* times? Let's just say that no one questioned his quirky ways. In fact, his methodology became known as the *HAL*-mark of the sport.

Zoey smiled at the bittersweet memories of her old coach. It was hard to believe that fourteen months had passed since his death. His passing had left a hole in her heart and an enormous void in the world of women's gymnastics. Worse, without Hal at the helm, the NGTC fell into complete and utter disarray. Once a well-oiled machine, there'd been no Plan B. Its illustrious thirty year history of producing world-class athletes came *this*close to ending with a shabby 'OUT OF BUSINESS' banner stretched across its doors.

That all changed when the mysterious Mr. Ash Harrington purchased it six months ago. In so doing, he'd rescued the renowned wellspring of elite gymnasts from tumbling into financial ruin.

Zoey squirmed, as she was wont to do at the thought – or sight—of the gym's new owner. Her mother used to complain that she'd come out of the womb strong-willed. She mustered that strength now to quash the roiling emotion, along with the heat that emanated outward and downward from the core of her being. She refused to acknowledge the sudden dampness in her panties. After all, it wasn't as if she held any allure for the infuriating man. Whereas her world tilted when he entered the room, he was oblivious to her existence. Other than a curt good morning or good evening, he seemed to avoid her whenever possible.

Was she so distasteful?

Zoey sucked back the last of the water, utterly disgusted with her mooning and swooning behavior in his presence. Her attraction to Ash Harrington was a one way commute down the Boulevard of Broken Dreams. Everyone knew it led straight off the well worn ledge of Ignored The Signs Bluff.

Even so, she was helpless to alter course. Drawn to the man as unerringly as a deer to headlights, Thelma and Louise had nuthin' on her!

Irked, she gnawed at her lower lip, not at all pleased with the lopsided status quo. Determined to change it, she didn't have a hot clue where to begin. When other girls were busy honing their female wiles, she was busy honing a double-back lay out with a two-and-a-half twist. Damn, that bitch was hard to stick.

In the ensuing years, she'd systematically tamped down whatever sexuality she may or may not have exuded.

Thanks to Billy Pickton...

Rejecting the shiver that began at the base of her spine and crawled across her scalp, Zoey sought out the sliver of mirror super-glued to the office wall. She wasn't unattractive, that much she knew. On the rare occasion she accompanied Gianna to a club, she received an inexplicable amount of attention from the opposite sex. Her roommate—who happened to be an exotic beauty who's parents still lived in Sicily—would stick out her bottom lip, feigning annoyance.

"Mio dio! I ask you, cara—-*why* do I torture myself?"

In return, Zoey would tease her, insisting that instead of Maria Chiara Alessandra – Gi's middle names should have been Drama Queen Extraordinara.

Peering past the layers of dust and fingerprints, Zoey took stock of her pale, freckle-spattered face. The individual features were ordinary enough, yet, somehow, they conglomerated into something quite striking. Especially her wide-set eyes. Dad always referred to them as 'Benton' green —a non-shade that encompassed everything from emerald to apple, depending on the light and the mood. At her present level of exhaustion, they registered as glassy jade.

Her favorite feature was the dimple at the corner of her mouth. She could live without the freckles, however.

Overall, not repulsive.

Not that it made a whit of difference. Bracing against the chair's screeching retort, Zoey adjusted her position, rolling onto one butt cheek in an attempt to alleviate the other. There was no escaping the fact that at the ripe old age of twenty-six, she'd spent most of her life in a gym. Sure, she'd dated a gymnast or two, but that was the extent of her social interaction with the opposite sex.

That is, except for Billy...

Shaking her head, she banished the vile name and the horrific night it invoked from her consciousness. She wrestled the nightmare back into the compartment it escaped from and locked it away where it belonged. To calm herself, she reached for her hair—a habit she'd developed as a result of that night and reinforced by the cataclysmic weeks that followed.

A decade later, playing with her hair was as second nature as breathing.

She pushed a tangle of the wayward locks from her forehead, knowing even as she tucked them away that the effort was in vain. The mass of soft ringlets had always proven unruly, mocking even professional attempts to tame them. Even now, after a long, hard day—the chestnut curls bounced back with the frenetic energy of a rock star on cocaine and Red Bull.

Running her fingers through them again and again, she sought the perfect strand to twirl and twist. Finding it, she picked up her lost train of thought. Now, where was she?

Oh, yes!
Ash Harrington...

Chapter 2

Naked and in complete darkness, he fed the 35mm film onto the reel and placed it in the developing tank. When it was safe to turn on the light, he jerked his rock-hard dick a few times before pouring in the chemicals.

"Stop distracting me. You know as well as I do that it takes time. Now, mind your manners!"

He spoke to his genitals more than he'd ever spoken to his wife.

Once the chemicals were added, he hovered over the tank like a mother hen, timer in one hand, errant cock in the other. Sweat poured from his arm pits, the odor so pungent it challenged the toxic chemicals for supremacy. There were six minutes and twenty seconds to endure until the next step, and there was no rushing it, despite his phallus' urging. Each step was crucial to the outcome.

Just thinking about the images coalescing in the tank had him vibrating on the brink of ejaculation.

Whatever the fuck 'normal' was? He was the furthest thing from. He didn't accept the fact, he embraced it. Of course, as a youngster, he'd tried to *feel* like other kids. Even then, he knew intuitively that it was hopeless. Amoral sociopaths with narcissistic tendencies and penchants for sadistic violence were just born different. The same as one guy was born black, another white.

It was nobody's fault, it was just the way the cosmic cards were dealt. And, from his entitled Caucasian perch above the sweaty masses, his hand looked mighty royal flush-y. Twiddling his quivering member, a grin stretched from ear to ear. Alone in the darkroom, there was no need to make adjustment to it, no need to hide the evil around the edges.

Like most soulless sociopaths, he was brilliant at affecting emotions, duplicating behaviors, and simulating compassion – otherwise known as pretending to give a shit. When they laughed, he pulled on a happy face and laughed along with them. When they were sad, he dug out his best sad face and became duly devastated. If the truth were known, Jack Nicholson would be kissing his hairy, yet talented ass. As early as grade two, he was perfecting facial expressions. He spent hours, days – *years*—in front of a mirror, twisting his features into award-winning replicas of emotions he could never feel.

Interest—*Check.*

Affection—*Check.*

Empathy—*Check, check.*

For the sake of simplicity, the emoticons he assumed most often were labeled, as were the more complex. Patient Listener was a fave. It took months to perfect, but was worth every second. Patient Listener alone had the power to get him all the free pussy he wanted, if free pussy was what he was after. It wasn't. Free pussy was boring as fuck.

DING!

His heart rate went through the roof. His forefinger spasmed, stopping the timer before the second ding. Forcing his hands to stop shaking, he cracked all ten knuckles before draining the chemical solution into the sink. Placing the tank under the faucet, he refilled it with fresh, one-hundred-degree water. In his mind's eye, he imagined the excess chemicals washing away from the twenty-four images within and giggled.

Soon...

Resetting the timer for three and a half minutes, he pick up his twerking dick and his grandiose thoughts where he'd left them.

Yes indeed, he was a master of disguise and duplicity, amongst other things. Charming, successful and rich, men wanted to be him and women wanted to fuck him. That is, until they found out his idea of a good time included drugging, raping, and – after a little more fun—choking the life out of them. Two had so much fun, they'd begged to die. Closing his eyes, he could almost hear them, their once sweet voices hoarse from screaming.

And the ligature, of course.

Without notice, his mind cartwheeled away from those precious memories to a young girl in a red gown. In his mind's eye, the useless whore was laughing. At him. The idea never failed to turn him apoplectic with rage. She'd been hand-picked to be his first, a well-deserved graduation gift to himself. Rushed and inexperienced, he'd forgotten to take her super-charged metabolism into account. He'd gotten the dosage wrong. While he managed to shove her dress up and get her panties off, when he went to stick his dick in, she began to wake up.

Luckily, he'd had the wherewithal to snip a lock of her hair before rearranging her clothing and plastering a concerned expression on his face.

That catastrophic failure became his driving force, determining his life choices. Over the years, he'd worked hard to perfect his craft. He looked forward to showing her just how far he'd come.

Soon, my lovely, soon...

Only his parents had an inkling as to the depths of his depravity. Early on, they realized they'd spawned seriously damaged goods. He'd hear them screaming late at night, each blaming the other for the 'monster' they'd created. Not that he'd given a shit, other than their racket made it difficult to get a good night's sleep. He'd never felt any connection to them. His instinct was to feed from them until he was glutted and they were gutted.

They split up after Cuddles, the family Pomeranian, disappeared. While the dog's body was never found, he'd missed a few tiny drops of blood on his cheek. He was only seven, after all. There was much to learn.

In any case, the looks on their faces were to die for. Literally.

After that, he ping-ponged between his broken, empty shell of a father and his alcoholic, whore of a mother. Both prayed the psychiatrist they sent him to could pull a Geppetto and turn him into a real boy. *As if.* At seventeen, he left with a boatload of scholarships and without a goodbye, never to look back. In the interim, they'd both kicked the bucket. He'd seen the obits.

Glancing at the stopwatch, a jolt of excitement raced through him. Unable to resist, he clicked it off seven seconds before it was set to buzz. His temples throbbed. White noise filled his head. It felt like he was moving through pea soup as he emptied the tank for the final time.

At last!

Reaching in, he removed the spool with more loving care than he'd ever shown another human being. He didn't even try to stop his hands from shaking as he attached a clip to the end and began to unwind the thread. The first image was enough to cause his balls to contract. Before he could move on to the second, white-hot ejaculate gushed into the conveniently located sink.

Still, his cock did not flag. *How could it?*

The girl on the negative was stunning, far more attractive in death than in life. He'd told her that would be the case as he was squeezing the last gasping breaths from her lungs. Looking closer, he patted himself on the back. He was never wrong about such things. Devouring her with his eyes, he licked his sandpaper dry lips much like he'd licked her clammy, white-as-a-sheet cheek mere moments before she'd expired.

Seeing her in lifeless repose, he recalled her name. *Roberta.* Yes, that was it—Roberta something or other. Just another worthless whore, like the rest of them.

This particular worthless whore lay spread-eagled and glassy-eyed in the ditch, her bushy pubis taking center stage. He could just make out her not-so-private parts, torn and bloodied from his vigorous ministrations. Countless ligature marks ringed her once porcelain throat, one for each instruction she didn't follow and, of course—one to help her on her way to a better place. The one thing Cuddles had taught him was that he had no taste for blood. He left such crudities to the Dahmer's and Gacy's of the world. He far preferred the ligature. An intimate dance of give and take, it required patience and a finesse few could master.

This slut had been great fun and great practice, a two-fer that brought him that much closer to his objective. When that day arrived, he planned to clear his calender...take his sweet time...

When his cock lurched in anticipation, he patted the

sticky head.

"Patience, my greedy comrade. It won't be long now. I promise."

His phone clattered on the countertop, interrupting his conversation. For a second, he considered ignoring it but quickly came to his senses.

"Daddy, are you coming home? Dinner's ready."

MOTHER FUCKING FUCK!

His only consolation was that the negatives would take hours to dry. His response was cursory.

"I'm on my way..."

Chapter 3

Undoing the button on her skort, Zoey wriggled her free hand under the waistband, allowing it to go where it wanted and do what it pleased. She wasn't surprised when it wound up cupping her sex, which in turn pulsated against the palm, swollen and sopping. The thought of Ash Harrington's wide brow, square jaw, and tight ass never failed to elicit a reaction. More often than not, that reaction culminated with a pair of viscous panties in the laundry and a fabulous night's sleep.

If she smoked, a cigarette would be standard operating procedure, as well.

But it was more than Ash's physical appearance that whetted her appetite and her underwear. Much more. Something within him touched something within her that she'd thought dead after Billy Pickton. She wasn't sure how he'd managed to bypass the maze of land mines and booby traps embedded around her heart, but somehow – he had. Such effortless breaching of her defenses set her mind to reeling and her juices to flowing.

Speaking of juices, Zoey pushed the panty's sodden crotch to one side. Dipping two fingers into her overflowing sex, she began to circle her dilated clit. Six months into their one-sided non-relationship, her desire to be close to him had only intensified. It made no sense, and yet, there it was. His presence soothed her soul, no hair twirling required. Zoey shuddered, thinking of the many times she'd come close to blurting out her feelings. Thank god she'd managed to contain herself. She could just imagine the pity in his eyes after he rebuffed her outright.

Still, there was that one day...

Frowning, Zoey recalled the day in question. Time slowed as her heart raced, just as it did then. There'd been something on his mind, she'd 'felt' the weight of it. She'd held her breath, her nipples tightening in anticipation of his words. Or, better yet—his actions. Alas, neither came to pass. As strong as the feeling was, it was nothing but wishful thinking on her part. Ash left the way he always did: with barely a glance in her direction.

PING!

The text notification was enough to startle her from her maudlin thoughts, but fell short of dislodging her hand from between her legs.

PING!

PING!

PING!

Even as a used up ex-gymnast, Zoey was still Gumby-flexible. In fact, her left shoulder was far more 'flexible' than was prudent, popping free of its socket with the slightest provocation. She could whack it back into place, of course, but it was the furthest thing from fun, leaving her bruised and nauseous for days. The career-ending injury served as a constant reminder of what might have been. Arching over the back of the chair, she snagged the strap of her purse with her good arm.

She already knew it was Gianna. Her effervescent roommate texted the same way she spoke – in rapid-fire bursts. She couldn't wait to hit the send button, creating an avalanche of single words and phrases.

PING!

PING!

Double tapping her phone, she read the incoming missives as they appeared.

Gi: *Mamma mia, Zee, this guy is HOT HOT HOT (heart, happy face)*

Gi: *Dying to tell you who he is...*

Gi: *But...*

Gi: *He said he'd have to kill me if I did...(lol, wink face)*

Gi: *You know what that means (sad face)*

Gi: *Married!*

Gi: *Ah, well...(sad face) Aren't they all? (lol, wink face)*

Gi: *He's coming back. Gotta go...*

Gi: *Ciao bella (heart, heart, happy face, heart)*

Shaking her head, Zoey saw no need to respond. She adored Gi like the sister she never had, she didn't judge. In fact, her penchant for married men aside, she envied her carefree friend, often living vicariously through her. Gianna lived life to the fullest whereas Zoey simply marked time, tormented by the past and pining for an unattainable future.

As Gianna would say: Ah, well...

Zoey's breath rasped into the silence as she resumed diddling herself. While her unrequited attraction to Ash was difficult to fathom, it was even harder to resist. With all the time in the world, she allowed her fingers to do the walking and her mind to do the talking.

The whole world knew who Ash 'The Oak' Harrington was. Built like your run of the mill brick shit house, the nickname spoke to how hard he was to cut down. The Oak had been a wrestling sensation since his junior high days. He'd caused quite the international kerfuffle when he pinned 'Mountain' Marek Kreveznik – the odds on favorite to crush his skull—to the Olympic mat and held him there for a hard count of three.

Armed with the coveted gold medal, Ash could have coasted all the way to the bank. Aside from endorsing his favorite brands of wrestling gear, Wheaties, Nike, and many others clamored for his attention. GM paid him an obscene amount to drive their high-end products around town. Versace even named a cologne after him. The ads were enough to get women – and men—to stop whatever they were doing and start drooling. *Harrington* was touted as 'a strong, masculine scent infused with a woodsy bouquet and irresistible base notes of musk'.

Mumbo jumbo aside, Zoey could vouch for the irresistible part.

Set for life, Ash wasn't content. Instead of enjoying the golden fruits of his labor, he once again hit the gym. Hard. Four years later, he repeated the incredible feat to bring home another Olympic gold and underscore his place in the history books.

And, the comic books.

Yes, there was even a comic book series dedicated to the wrestling superhero. It sat on the same shelf as The Hulk and Chief Marvel.

All of this was public knowledge. His personal life, however, was not. Obsessed with privacy, conjecture and speculation swirled. Zoey had pieced together what she could. He'd been married, that much she knew. His ex-wife, Mercedes, visited the gym so infrequently that enquiring tongues were wont to wag. After all, their daughter, Cherish, was an up and coming gymnast, already garnering attention on the world stage at the pivotal age of thirteen.

When the ex-Mrs. Harrington *did* make an appearance,

you could cut the tension with a butter knife. She checked the time often, more often if her ex-husband was around. She avoided him like the plague, not bothering to hide her vexation at his presence. She never stayed long. Rumor had it that after thirteen years of wedded bliss she'd filed for an annulment, citing fraud. Failing that, she'd settled for a divorce.

It was said that he bought the failing NGTC just to get more face time with his daughter. With enough profitable investments and endorsements to choke a gift horse, he certainly didn't need the losing proposition.

What he did in the name of fatherly love touched Zoey's heart, making her yearn for him even more. After all, one out of every two marriages wound up in divorce. Who was she or anybody else to judge? Revving up her moisture-logged fingers, she envisioned her beloved's face as she worked herself into a lather. At this rate, she'd be home in no time.

Teetering on the edge of self-gratification, a muffled thud stayed her hand. High-strung at the best of times, she admonished herself to stay calm. The massive old building moaned and groaned all the time, as did the sea of equipment that filled it. That being said, this noise was different. Orgasm forgotten, Zoey pulled her hand from her crotch and leaned forward. Squinting, she peered past the office door and into the shadows of the deserted main gym. Nothing seemed amiss. Chalk dusk hung in the air, sparkling in the dimness. Armed, the light on the alarm glowed a steady, comforting red.

Feeling a wee bit silly, she shook off the unwarranted willies and stood. Using both hands, she kneaded the knots in her aching back, groaning with sweet relief. It was time to head home, no more dilly-dallying. She'd call her mother, take a hot bath and read a little. She'd discovered erotic romance several months back and loved it – the grittier the better.

Zoey's face burned with that harsh truth. Right or wrong, the Dominant/submissive themed love stories spoke to her Dominant/submissive themed soul. Kinky sex aside, the power exchange component reminded her of the relationship between a coach and a high-level athlete.

Without question, Hal had been the nucleus of her existence. He'd held her life in his hands—literally. He alone dictated what she ate, when she slept, what marks she was expected to get in school. He kept track of her height and weight – to the quarter-inch and ounce. A disapproving glance could trigger tears of desolation. The hint of a smile would fill her world with sunshine and rainbows. Not a day passed that he didn't push her to exceed her limits. The only thing she needed to worry about was improving. Hal looked after everything else.

She'd often wondered if the submissive was drawn to the gym, or if the gym helped create the submissive. It was the age old question of which came first, the chicken or the egg. There were strong philosophical arguments on both sides, yet no definitive answer.

Add in the kinky sex, however, and there was no grey area. Zoey would fall asleep dreaming of bondage and blindfolds – and worse – oh, my. Without exception, she and Ash Harrington played the starring roles.

With a hot date with a hot book to look forward to, she collected her purse and keys. Sighing, she shrugged into her coat. There was no escaping the fact that she chose to lose herself in fiction and fantasy rather than face the sad reality of her own life.

The instant she switched off the office lights, all hell broke loose. The front doors flew open a split second before the alarm began to wail, lights flashing madly. Tightening the muscles in her bad shoulder, she prepared to protect herself. She may be small, but she was fast, flexible, and feisty. If all else failed, she knew the cavernous gymnasium like the back of her hand. There was a myriad of places to hide until the police could get there.

After Billy, she was determined to never again be a victim. She'd rather die.

With the lights out, she crept out of the office, hoping that the alarm had scared whoever it was away. Her heart sank when she saw the hulking figure in the doorway.

She couldn't contain the scream that formed in the pit of her stomach and rose to fill her throat...

Chapter 4

Ash made a conscious effort to unclench his jaw. With Mercedes weighing heavy on his mind, the simple task required a grit reminiscent of his wrestling days. The loft he'd rented after their divorce had a long central hallway. In a little under a year, he'd paced the once-glossy finish from the maple floorboards. Every now and again, he paused to stare out the enormous plate-glass window at the hall's far end. It reached almost to the exposed rafters, an impressive conduit for sunshine and light. The golf course it overlooked was lush and serene, a sprawling study in green.

Or...*greens.*

All punning aside, Ash hardly noticed. Locked in a now-familiar world of self-loathing, he was blind to the beauty that surrounded him. To say that he blamed himself for the breakup of his marriage was an understatement of biblical proportion. Guilt gnawed at his gut and tortured his mind, a despised yet constant companion. He bore the mantle of responsibility as a monk bore a hairshirt – without a word of complaint. After all, he deserved to suffer. And who better to mete out the punishment than himself? He did so on a daily basis and with a vengeance.

His ever-deepening frown lines attested to the fact. Catching a glimpse of his reflection in the window, he turned away, choosing to not make eye contact. He was all too familiar with the weary self-condemnation he would find there. Looking at himself in the mirror was something he did as little as possible these days.

Instead, he went to take a piss. The picture window

wasn't the only attraction at the end of the hall.

Relieving himself in long, satisfying squirts, Ash watched the toilet water roil against the stuttering impact and thought once again of his ex. There was no doubt that, in him, she'd gotten a raw deal. He'd conceded the fact long before the divorce papers were served. He conceded it still. She married a gentle, inexperienced boy and wound up with an aggressive, libidinous man. Worse yet, the aggressive, libidinous man had an insatiable appetite for bondage, spankings and more.

How was she to foresee such a despicable transformation?

Come to think of it – how was he? Ash flushed the commode with one hand, shaking the last few droplets from his dick with the other. With full intent, he left the toilet seat up. It was foolish, of course, yet he maintained the symbolic 'fuck you' on behalf of whipped men everywhere. With that lofty mission accomplished, it was time for a cocktail.

The loft, bless its designer's heart, came with a games room replete with an ornate bar. Stepping around the pool table and behind the curved conversation piece, he ignored the pyramid of glass shelves crammed with fancy bottles. Crouching, he instead selected his libation from the mini-fridge. Since leaving his champagne and caviar wife, he'd developed a taste for beer, preferring foreign to domestic. Cracking open an ice cold Heineken, he swigged straight from the bottle, then waited for the long, satisfying belch that was sure to follow.

Health conscience his whole life, Ash wasn't much of a drinker. With the discipline of ten men and a small boy, he had little respect for those who over-indulged. On the other hand, an occasional beer was a great way to disrupt his self-flagellation – a far more dangerous pastime, indeed.

It wasn't until their eighth year of wedding bliss that he'd discovered his penchant for dominance. It'd laid inert for twenty-nine years as he gained enough knowledge and insight to manage it. Once unleashed, it was like a tidal wave – unstoppable and all-consuming. It seemed to emanate from his very soul, a critical component of his DNA.

Ash sighed. It was as hard to explain as it was to contain.

He knew. He'd tried both. Had he succeeded at either, he'd probably still be married. As Mercedes so eloquently put it, he was just plain 'fucked-up' – a 'twisted sicko' who needed to go directly to counseling. There was no time to pass 'GO' and he didn't deserve to collect two hundred dollars.

Ash didn't disagree, in spite of the devilish grin that pulled at the corners of his lips. After all, he'd only spend the money on rope.

"What's happened to you, Ash? Where's the shy, sweet man I married?"

"He grew up, Merc. He discovered himself. Is that so bad? I didn't hear you complaining last night. Matter of fact, what I heard was you screeching through what looked like a pretty fine orgasm. Or, should I say – orgasms, plural. It *was* a multiple, was it not, darling?"

"You're a beast to mention such a thing. It's not like I'm given a choice, bound and blindfolded as you've come to prefer. I'm complaining now. That's what matters."

"What matters is that you *like* it and you *know* it. Why can't you just admit it?"

And so it went. Back and forth. Every day for five long years. And then, one day—it stopped. It was the day he'd introduced a pair of clover leaf nipple clamps and she'd orgasmed for twenty minutes straight. As it turned out, it was the most miserable day of his life. Upon descent from her multi-orgasmic high, she freed her clamped nipples and headed straight for her lawyer.

His guilt meant that she got the house, the art collection, the condo in Cannes, a seven-digit lump sum settlement—and thousands in monthly spousal support. When that wasn't enough, she contended that his 'disgusting perversions' were a result of a concussion he'd suffered as a wrestler. Somehow, irreparable brain damage sat dormant for decades before manifesting itself in the form of deviant sexual behavior so extreme, she wasn't able to speak of it.

A barrage of sworn statements to the courts meant that she also got the kid, and thousands more a month. The money meant nothing, but his daughter? His little monkey? Ash grunted as though he'd been sucker punched. Pulling up a bar stool, he all but collapsed onto it. He and Cherish had always been tight. At thirteen, she was the best of both her parents, combining her mother's looks and grace with his strength and determination. He'd bought the gym to be closer to her. While that was working out great, there were other issues related to the purchase. Disconcerting issues.

Issues that had nothing to do with snatching it from the jaws of financial ruin...

Chapter 5

Ash frowned, his form-fitting jeans pulling in all the wrong places. Adjusting himself, he knew all too well the reason for his sudden turgidity.

Zoey Benton...

That little enchantress had cast a spell on him the moment they'd met. She'd caught him unawares, defenses down. Six months later, and, still, he could not stop thinking about her. Her sexy voice. Her unguarded laugh. Her irresistible scent.

Those freckles...

Cutting off the direction of his thought, he took a vicious swig from the bottle. After the implosion of his marriage and the adjacent shame that came along with it, he'd vowed to stay the fuck away from women. He had no desire to impose his 'disgusting perversions' on an unsuspecting opposite sex. Especially those of the sweet and innocent variety.

Like Zoey...

Ash shook his head. With a single glance, the fathomless depths of her eyes had pinned him to the proverbial mat.

"It's such an honor to meet you, sir. I've read so much about you. And, obviously, your daughter didn't fall far from the tree. I adore Cherish. She's going places, I can tell."

Her small hand resting in his made it difficult to concentrate on her words, kind as they were. All he knew was that a red-hot need was racing from where their flesh met straight to his dick, taking an unscheduled detour through his heart. Struck dumb by the force, he managed to mutter some drivel in response before turning away, her aquamarine eyes tattooed onto the backsides of his eyelids.

She must have thought him an arrogant boor. In truth, the protruding tent in his pants was as obvious then as it was today. The poor girl would have had a stroke if she'd gotten a gander.

Mercedes had done her level best to eviscerate him. She'd sliced and diced him up pretty good, starting with his psyche and working her way down. Yet, where Zoey was concerned, his penis disregarded the memo, taking an 'erect' stance on the matter and never wavering.

Again, he adjusted himself, his cock continuing to swell despite his chagrin. As a distraction, he concentrated on dates, times and places instead of the depth of her eyes or the curve of her luscious lips. He knew all about Zoey Benton's celebrated gymnastics career of a decade ago. He'd been married with a three year old back then, out of training for several years. Nonetheless, as an ex-Olympian, he'd kept his finger on the pulse.

Lean and mean, young Zoey was more reminiscent of Olga than Mary Lou, although her light-up-the-sky smile conjured images of both. She threw one-of-a-kind tricks with a combination of devil-may-care abandon and dead-on accuracy—making her an odds on favorite to earn a spot on 'The Team'. The Benton Twist was named after her. Even today, very few attempted her high-flying, signature move.

Fans ate her up. Judges adored her. She was spoken of in terms of when, not if. And then...something happened.

While nobody knew the exact details, whatever it was culminated in a change in personality, a loss of confidence – and, finally—a career-ending injury. A dislocated shoulder was a bitch to heal, the tissue and tendons surrounding it ripped to shit. It left her on the sidelines, a forgotten footnote in history. The old injury still gave her problems, he could tell.

Fast forward a decade. The failed gymnast grew into a woman so beautiful, she could have her choice of runways from New York to Milan. Her sweet laughter and giving nature made her all the more alluring. Yet, she'd never strayed from the place where her dreams were built, and, ultimately—destroyed. Somehow, she didn't have a clue how stunning she was.

The problem was, he did.

There was no accounting for the effect she had on him, yet, effect him she did. In a *big* way. Squirming in discomfort, he popped the button on his jeans. The pressure from within was so great, the fly almost unzipped itself. Unfolding his bloated cock, he maneuvered it from the waistband of his briefs. Alignment restored, he returned to nursing his beer, doing his best to ignore the throbbing organ. It was no small feat. The demand for attention began in his balls and oozed from the tip. With a finger, he caught a globule of pre-cum before it could spill onto the floor, then wiped it on the leg of his jeans.

While he'd done everything in his power to avoid her, he was, in the end, only human. Wincing, he recalled the day he'd almost swept her into his arm and told her how he really felt. He'd convinced himself that her eyelashes batted for his attention, that her chocolate curls bounced for his pleasure. He'd gone so far as to lift a hand, intent on running his fingers through them. Pulling it back in the nick of time, he'd turned on his heel and left the room without a word. The surprise on her face was as apparent as the scowl on his.

He'd had a weak moment, that was all. After Mercedes, he'd determined to never again expose his true nature and thereby risk another painful rejection. There was no need for him to spend so much time at the NGTC. He had offices across the city – across the country, in fact.

Yet, his resolve was hobbled when confronted with the yearning in his soul. Not to mention, the hard-on in his pants. Even his best wrestling moves, the Wizzer and the Gazzoni, were useless against the killer combination. Six months after their first meeting, his attraction to the ex-gymnast stood resolute. Again, much like the unflagging pole in his pants.

That's enough!

Disgusted with himself, he rose from the bar-stool, finished the last dregs of beer and wiped his mouth. He had a hankering to burn off some steam and it just so happened that his newest acquisition was equipped with a state-of-the-art weight room. The NGTC was barely a hop and a skip from where he lived, and at this hour, it would be deserted. A jog would do him good. He forced his member back from whence it had risen and went to change.

Hurrying to outpace his thoughts, he shoved his wallet, keys and phone into the various pockets of his reflective slicker and hit the road. While the fresh air felt great, it did little to clear his mind. Churning, it had no problem keeping up with his pumping legs.

Once upon a time, he'd paid to have his fantasies fulfilled. He wasn't ashamed to admit it. What he *was* ashamed to admit was the disastrous outcome. After failing to get up what today he couldn't get down—he'd understood that not only was he a twisted motherfucker, he was a twisted motherfucker that needed to feel connected to the woman he dominated. It meant nothing with a stranger.

Long story short, he was sentenced to a lifetime of solitary confinement, masturbation, and fantasy.

With that sad fact as stimulus, Ash kicked up the pace a notch from brutal to punishing. He pulled the hood up against the light rain that was falling, making a game of jumping puddles. In no time, he was standing at the gym's modest main entrance, searching for keys and the pass code to the alarm system. He'd tucked it safely away in his wallet.

Somewhere...

Pulling his XXXL hand from an XL pocket, he managed to drop the keys. The night was dark, the lighting poor. Making a mental note to call the security company in the morning, he bent down to search the concrete near his feet. In so doing, his shoulder slammed into the doors so hard, it left a dent.

In the doors.

Feeling no pain but pissed nonetheless, he located the keys and whipped open the offending door, using frustration as impetus. It crashed against the inside wall just as the alarm began to shrill. If that wasn't enough, there was something else adding to the bedlam. Squinting into the darkness, a figure in the hallway caught his eye. With the reflexes of a cat, he crouched, prepared for anything.

Well...almost anything.

What he wasn't prepared for was a terrified Zoey, screaming as though she'd just seen a ghost...

Chapter 6

"Zoey? Zoey, is that you? What the hell are you doing here, girl?"

Just as she was willing herself to turn and run, the sound of Ash's voice relieved her of the burden. Despite her earlier bravado, she'd found herself rooted to the spot, jello-legged and screaming like a lunatic. The shock of the moment had unleashed a flashback to a nightmare she'd struggled to forget for a decade.

"Stop that hollering girl. It's me, Ash Harrington. I just stopped by to use the weight room."

"Mr. Harrington? Thank god! Yes, yes, it's me, Zoey. I worked late and must have lost track of the time."

Her next words slipped out unwarranted, no doubt due to the wave of relief washing over her.

"I'm so glad you're here, sir."

"Call me Ash. Are you alright, girl?"

She was better than alright. She was floating on air.

"I'm so glad you're here. Ash..."

The dim light from the parking lot framed his massive silhouette as he strode toward her. His dark hair glistened, his thigh muscles bulged. A sight for sore eyes, she gobbled him up, stopping just short of smacking her lips. The way he moved caused the muscles in her belly to contract, most notably when he was moving in her direction. His natural confidence left her panting, his eyes locking into hers rendered her breathless. Fear drained from her body, leaving plenty of room for its equally powerful replacement: Desire.

Mixed with a double jolt of adrenaline and a triple shot

of exhaustion, it was a knee-buckling concoction, indeed. Zoey floated within her own body, the universe in a slow motion holding pattern.   Instead of muscle and bone to support her, there was half a year's worth of hopes and horniness.   Converted into rocket fuel, it was more than enough to get to the moon. And back.

Zoey smiled first at the image, then at the man to whom her soul beckoned.   She thought of the stacks of erotic romance novels she'd read, substituting herself as the submissive heroine and Ash as the Dominant hero.   This wasn't like any of them.

Happening in real time, this was so much better...

But, when he veered off script to punch the code into the alarm system and call the provider, Zoey mentally kicked her own ass. *What the hell was wrong with her?* How many times did he have to reject her before she finally got the memo? Flushing, humiliation prickled her skin.   She looked to her feet, searching for words to cover her embarrassment.   What she found was her ire.   The dumbass clearly didn't know a good thing when he saw it.   Nor, when it threw itself at his feet.

The silence after the din was deafening.   Running on fumes and adrenaline, she looked up, a piece of her mind on the tip of her tongue. Somehow, they were nose to nose, mere inches apart. He'd covered the remaining space between them with the silence and precision of a cruise missile.

And the impact? *Devastating!*

A mushroom cloud of unadulterated lust blanketed her. Gasping, she inhaled his exhale, hot and heavy from exertion. She filled her lungs with his essence, a mixture of damp clothes, stale beer, and pheromones powerful enough to melt the most stalwart of undergarments. Up close and personal, she memorized his every feature, many of them criss-crossed with scars.

His hair was damp. Normally pushed straight back, dark tendrils of it fell across his forehead. It was all she could do to not reach out and sweep them aside. Beads of sweat and rain ran down his throat, soaking the neckline of his shirt. Zoey's mouth watered. With pleasure, she'd have caught each and every droplet with her tongue. Past the point of decorum, she ogled his Adam's apple and licked her lips. Dragging her gaze upwards, she was caught in the twin oceans that were his eyes. Giving herself over to both tide and current, she opened her soul for his perusal.

"My beautiful little seductress, what spell have you cast?"

His words took a moment to register. When they did, their import hit her full-force, causing her knees to finally buckle. Ash's arm was right there to catch her. Wrapping it nearly all the way around her, he pulled her hard against him. Emphasis on hard. The phallus palpitating her belly was no small matter, as shocking in dimension as the man that held her. Zoey's head swam at his nearness. Tears of joy welled in her eyes just as her juices breached the gathered hem of her panties and began to seep down her thighs.

When he spoke again, his voice was low, almost guttural. A tic played at the corner of his mouth, a vein throbbed at his temple. For a moment, he looked angry. She wasn't even sure if he was talking to her – or to himself.

"How is it possible that some...some *chit* of a girl can make me throw caution to the wind and...and..."

And...really, what else was there to say? Even the mighty 'Oak' couldn't defend against destiny.

Still moving, his lips took hers, almost with a vengeance. They scraped against hers, demanding a response. Willingly, she gave it, rising on tip-toe to offer more. For a fleeting second, his hard edges softened and she tasted the exquisite truth. Ash wanted her as much as she wanted him. When he tore his lips from hers, she moaned, bereft.

"Please, please...I've waited...wished..."

She was making no sense and she knew it. Her blood was boiling, rushing in a direction a hundred and eighty degrees opposite to her brain. She squirmed, trying to reach his lips—impossible if he didn't bend to meet her. She realized she was grinding her pelvis against him just a moment too late. She felt the growl in his chest before it burst from his throat.

"Be careful what you whimper for, my sweet."

His free hand flew up. Running it through her hair, he helped himself to a handful, wrapping the thick curls around his thicker fist. With the first tug, she stopped squirming. With the second, she very nearly came. The shocking realization was like a jab to the solar plexus. Her jaw dropped almost to her chest.

"You've poked the sleeping bear this evening, my dear. As you can see – and feel – you've earned my full attention. Now, seeing as how your mouth is already hanging open, please stick out your tongue."

Stick out her tongue?

Her gasp pierced the cacophonous silence his words left behind. Surely, she'd misheard? If not, the surreal request was slow to sink in. A third tug to her hair sped the process up considerably. Squealing, she poked the tip of her tongue just past her teeth and looked up to him for approval. Other than a sardonic smile, his features were inscrutable. His eyes glinted like a hypnotist's pendulum, the irises deeper than quick sand. There was no sign of the inner struggle she'd sensed earlier. Ash Harrington was in complete control of himself. And, of her.

Thrilled with her plight, Zoey awaited his pleasure, tongue out and pussy spasming.

"Are you begging to be spanked, babygirl? Hmmm...? Trust me, it would be my pleasure, so I suggest you not tempt me further. Now, please stick out your tongue. And this time —all the way!"

The idea that he might actually spank her served as excellent motivation. Cheeks aflame, she extended her tongue so far, the base ached and her mouth watered. In seconds, saliva was spilling from the tip.

"That's my good girl. Perfect. Now, judging from the rock-hard nipples drilling into my chest, your little cunt must be drenched. Am I right, Zoey? Is your little cunt drenched? Hmmm...?"

Zoey was quite literally gobsmacked. If Ash weren't holding her up, she'd be flat on ass, guaranteed. Never in her life had she heard that word spoken aloud, yet, he uttered it as nonchalantly as one might comment on the weather. He couldn't possibly expect her to answer?

Could he?

Seconds ticked by. Zoey's mind reeled. Her clit twanged. She didn't dare retract her tongue.

"Yeth, thir. Dwentht."

"I'm sorry, darling? What's drenched?"

Teetering on the edge of sub-space, Zoey did what came naturally: she submitted to the will of the man she adored.

"Cunth. Cunth dwentht thir."

His proud smile was ear-to-ear. Equally proud, she swooned in his arms.

"You don't mind if I double check, just to be sure?"

This time, he didn't wait for an answer. Disentangling his hand from her hair, he reached between her legs and waited. Zoey understood and was eager to accommodate. She parted her thighs, allowing his hand entry. His chuckle sealed her fate.

When his lips descended upon hers for the second time, her dripping, distended tongue collided with his, joining in a dance as old as time. It was only natural that her arms wound around his neck, her fingers finding the thick bands of muscle she'd yearned for so long to knead. Fused to him mind, body and soul, she'd never felt so soft. So safe. So secure.

And, SO fucking horny!

Evidence of their escalating ardor echoed back at them—a stirring duet of low-pitched grunts and high-pitched whimpers. As Maestro, Ash plucked her strings at will. Over top of her panties, his forefinger traced the length of her slit. When at last it came to rest on her bulging, throbbing clit, Zoey was undone.

With one expert tap, a Category Five orgasm ripped through her, blowing her mind and shaking her to the core...

Chapter 7

We, The People
by Gabriel Montero

SECOND GYMNAST FOUND MURDERED?

Zoey squinted at the headline, a ball of masticated toast sticking mid-way down her gullet. Salvaging the one drop of saliva left in her mouth, she winced and swallowed hard. With her throat cleared of the multi-grained obstacle, there was plenty of room for her hammering heart. Her carotid arteries bulged in an attempt to manage the sudden onslaught of blood and adrenaline.

Failing that, her head spun, her ears rang, and her skin crawled. There was a fifty-fifty chance she was going to yak into her bowl of strawberries and fat free Cool Whip. There was no use fighting the vertigo. Trying to would only make it worse. All she could do was stare at her tablet until the nausea receded and the words shimmered back into focus.

When they did, they hadn't changed.

SECOND GYMNAST FOUND MURDERED?

She felt Gianna's eyes boring into her from across the table and read aloud. Or, tried to. Her voice emerged a cracked whisper. It came from the bottom of a dry well a zillion light years away. Taking a sip of orange juice for lubrication, she tried again.

Is a psychopath on the loose in our city? One who has a depraved appetite for athletes? Gymnasts, to be specific.

40

While the name of last night's victim has yet to be released, there's concern that a killer may be trolling for his victims in a very small, very elite pond. Discovered in a drainage ditch near Morning Acres farms, her body was displayed in the same unspeakable manner as Shondra (Jersey) Stefanson's just five months ago. When you put the two together, they have all the earmarks of a sadistic serial killer.

Although still unconfirmed, sources are whispering that the latest victim was well known in the highest echelons of women's gymnastics.

As was Shondra.

Unblinking, Zoey raised her eyes to meet Gianna's. The horror she found there could only mirror her own. They'd both trained with Jersey for a short time years before. While her brutal death had rocked them, the sport, *and* the nation— no one imagined there was a serial killer on the loose.

Zoey lowered her gaze and continued reading before her roommate caught a glimpse of her transparent thoughts.

Who can forget the morning Shondra's naked body was discovered in an open field off the I-75. There'd been no attempt to cover or bury her. At the time, it was rumored that the scene was staged, that she'd been lewdly 'posed' – a possible indicator of a serial killer acting out his sick and twisted fantasy. Five months later and these gruesome contentions are yet to be officially confirmed by the investigators.

We asked Chief Percy O'Malley. What we got in response

was the all-too-familiar O'Malley grunt of impatience along with the standard: That's absurd, Gabriel! We release information to the media and the public as it becomes available and is prudent.

Okie dokie, Chief.

What we do know, ladies and gentlemen, is this: The cause of Shondra's death was ligature strangulation. She'd been bound, raped and sodomized at an unknown location. The drainage ditch was a dump site, not the scene of the crime. No semen or fingerprints were recovered. The ligature was removed and taken from the scene. To date, there hasn't been a single arrest and just as many answers for the grieving family and community.

If this latest murder is connected, hide your children and bolt your doors – chances are we have a monster in our midst. A monster who's obsessed with detail and is very good at covering his tracks.

Stay tuned, loyal readers.

This bloodhound has caught a scent and intends to follow it until We, the People have all the facts.

"What is happening, cara?"

The panic in Gianna's voice helped Zoey to get a hold of herself. Despite freezing the night before, she still believed she could take care of herself herself, on the short term at least. Last night didn't count. After all, seeing the hulking figure in the doorway was the first time she'd felt threatened since...

Well, it was the first time she'd felt threatened in ten years.

Last night had ended up a dream come true, but, it could easily have turned out otherwise. She didn't expect there to be a next time, but she intended to be better prepared – just in case. Her mind snapped to the poor girl who'd been attacked in the night. *Please, please don't let it be a gymnast.* The implications would be staggering.

Shaking off the morbid thought, she half-smiled across the table at her best friend. She reinforced her voice with a quavering note of bravado, hoping it didn't come across as falsetto as it felt.

"Listen, Gi, as awful as it is, it's probably random. They don't know that it's a gymnast. You know as well as I do that the crime rate in this city is off the charts. I say we not worry about something that isn't a fact yet, whadda ya think?"

Gi's beautiful face seemed even thinner than usual, a sign that she was either 'in love' – or her eating disorder was back. Zoey prayed it was the former but feared it was the latter. An unspoken epidemic in the world of gymnastics, bulimia had forced Gianna from the sport at the height of her career, her very life on the line. At eighty-four pounds and dropping, she'd been unable to metabolize even the most meager of sustenance. What little went down came straight back up – no hands required.

Instead of taking her place on an Olympic podium, she took her place on a hospital ward, followed by months in rehab. From there, she'd moved into Zoey's second bedroom, oblivious to the trauma she'd experienced in her absence. Gianna credited Zoey with helping to nurse her back to health.

The truth was, they'd helped each other.

Today, Gianna's cheekbones looked ready to tear through the skin stretched across them. The broken blood vessels were almost indiscernible against her cafe au lait complexion, but even expertly applied make-up couldn't hide them from Zoey's educated eye. They spoke volumes, as did the yellow tinge to the whites of her eyes.

This wouldn't be Gi's first slip up, sadly. So far, she'd always managed to check herself before the insidious disease could consume her. Nonetheless, Zoey made a mental note to call Mama Ricci and Dr. Stillwater.

"I'm thinking we hit the mall, do some shopping, maybe see what's playing at the CinemaPlex. I've been dying to see that new X-rated romance everybody's talking about. Mastered, I think it's called. You in, girlfriend?"

With that tempting offer on the table, Gi's furrowed brow lifted just a smidge. The clouds in her eyes lightened. They did not clear. She offered a compromise.

"I can't do the movie today, cara mia, but, I'm all in for shopping. Maybe I can find something sexy to wear for my date with..."

Zoey could literally hear Gianna's jaws snap shut as she cut herself off. It wasn't in her nature to keep secrets, especially when it concerned the merry-go-round of men in her life. As a rule, she'd burble about them ad nauseum, delving deep and often into the 'Too Much Information' department. To hide her consternation, Zoey got up and began clearing the table. They'd been each others most trusted confidantes since they'd shared a dorm room and dreamed of competing together in the Olympics. While

44

they'd both fallen short, their friendship never wavered.

And now, there was something Gianna was keeping from her. Something to do with her new man – her new, *married* man. A cold tentacle of foreboding slithered up Zoey's spine. Seemingly unwarranted, it would not be marginalized. To escape its clutches, she pirouetted away from the table. Shaking off the willies, she gave herself a good talking to.

Who was she to judge? Especially when she kept a dark secret of her own.

Even after all these years, the 'incident' with Billy Pickton was still blurred around the edges, shot through with psychedelic streaks of denial and burning unanswered questions. One minute she'd been the happiest girl on earth— Cinderella on the arm of Prince Charming. The next she'd been doubled over, heaving her guts out without any idea what happened.

Her rumpled dress and panties spoke to something horrific. Billy's concerned voice and compassionate eyes said something completely different. Young and confused, she'd accepted his helping hand, applauded his crowning as Prom King, and stood back as a lovestruck gaggle of girls worshipped the ground he walked on.

Watching them fall at his feet, she'd felt more than a little silly. The biggest man on campus could have his pick of eager and willing debutantes – in multiples, it appeared. He didn't need to accost someone while they were rendered unawares. No doubt, she'd just fainted from a combination of excitement and champagne.

Her gut roiled in disagreement. It wasn't until she got home that she noticed the missing chunk of hair. It'd been chopped off at the scalp. From that day forward she refused to take his calls. The one message she listened to convinced her to not listen to a second. Alternating between wheedling pleas and seething anger, the wild swings in temperament were frightening. He signed off with a chilling farewell: *You're a worthless whore. Just like the rest of them...*

Her lack of response seemed only to encourage him. The calls kept coming, long after he'd left for college and she'd changed her number.

Twice.

She'd been jittery at best, at worst a full-blown wreck. Her concentration slipped. And then, one day, so did she. She should have stretched more, of course. And, she would have if her mind hadn't been otherwise occupied. She'd always had trouble with that shoulder, especially on bars. Moreso when bars was her first event. To this day, she could hear the *POP* her shoulder made as the bone tore free from its moorings.

Sighing, Zoey gnawed her lip. Hers was just one more sad story in an abyss of sad stories. The bottom line was that she'd never mentioned any of it to Gianna. How could she explain it to anybody else when she couldn't explain it to herself? She hoped to one day reconcile the damage that single date had wreaked on her life. But, that day wasn't today. And, it probably wasn't tomorrow, either.

Balancing her bowl on top of her glass, she succeeded in making it to the sink without incident. Gianna joined her, giggling at her spasmodic, graceless display. Still, an awkward silence persisted as they rinsed their dishes and stacked them in the dishwasher.

It was almost a relief when they went their separate ways to get dressed...

Chapter 8

Up close and personal, he watched the life fade to black in her unblinking, terrified eyes. Reveling in his supreme power to extinguish life, his rubber-protected dick exploded unaided, his seed streaming into the third extra-strength condom he'd filled in just over an hour. Slipping it from his withering member, he tied it off and slid it into the windbreaker's pocket to join the others.

Not bad. Not bad at all. This one wasn't much of a challenge, but, hey—he couldn't complain. The bitch put up a valiant struggle when and where it counted most, her abject terror keeping him happy and hard. The look on her face when she awoke bound and naked with her own panties twisted around her throat and him gnawing at a responsive nipple? Priceless.

Which reminded him...

Taking the disposable camera from his 'goody bag', he snapped off the last two pictures. The thought of developing the roll caused his spent dick to twitch in anticipation. Smiling, he imagined the horror he captured when she opened her mouth to welcome his leaking cock. 'Welcome' was a slight exaggeration, perhaps. He'd had to twist the ligature at her throat more than once before she'd seen the light and gobbled him to his hairy nutsack.

Not that he'd minded. In fact, it'd been his pleasure.

Refusing to climax in her mouth, he had her roll onto her belly while he pulled on the rubber, not a simple task wearing elbow-length neoprene gloves. He enjoyed fucking them up their usually virgin assholes first, all the time promising to let them go if they take it like a 'good girl'. In truth, sodomy was merely an appetizer. The gourmet meal to come included an entree of pain and humiliation with a delicious dollop of death for dessert.

Death hadn't always been on the menu. It was added after a near-disaster. He'd been living off campus, perfecting his technique with the all the fervor one would expect from a young, hot-blooded, sexual predator. As will happen in the throes of youthful passion, one evening he pushed his luck a little too far. The cunt ran to the campus cops ranting that he'd raped her, amongst other delectable deeds. Luckily, her reputation as campus slut preceded her, as did his of angelic golden boy. No report was filed. The campus slut transferred schools.

Ah, well...

It wasn't long after that he dropped out of college, reverted to his formal given name and legally adopted his mother's maiden name. With a little help from a plastic surgeon who favored money over ethics, Billy Pickton disappeared just as William Waters emerged – clean as a whistle and lessons well learned.

As fate would have it, snuffing the life from his victims became the central theme around which his array of sexual fantasies revolved. It was the crescendo to a hedonistic symphony of humiliation and torture.

As his current victim was about to find out...

Always thinking ahead, he'd bound her wrists behind her back. With some encouragement, she was able to spread her well-muscled ass-cheeks and invite him to violate her. He loved the horror in her voice as he instructed her on what to say, word for word. Although it was impossible to understand with all the sobbing and snivelling, he still had her repeat it over and over.

"Pu-pu-p-leez (gasp) p-p-pleas (wheeze) fu-fu-fuck (choke) m-m-my a-a-ssss (wail)..."

Music to his ears.

"Again, whore! Make me believe it."

When he was done reaming their assholes, there wasn't much fight left in them. It was unfortunate, but that's just the way it was. By the time he flipped them onto their backs to enjoy them in the more traditional style, they were all but unrecognizable. Eyes vacant and frothing at the mouth, the last one actually engaged in a heartfelt conversation with her deceased grandmother. Even if he allowed the worthless whores to live, they'd never leave the looney bin.

Killing them was doing them a favor.

Taking note of the time, he began to clean up. While he'd have liked to bring her back a time or two more, he was under tight constraints this night. His alibi was only good for so many hours, and he was a careful man. He hefted the broken body into his arms, removed the panty garrotte from around her neck and dumped her into the plastic lined trunk. Slamming it shut, he tucked himself in and straightened his clothes before sliding behind the wheel.

Checking his hair in the rear view mirror, he was pleased to find not a single strand out of place. There was more to be said for a military cut than just great style. Clicking the remote, he backed slowly out of the extra-large, sound-proofed storage locker he'd rented years ago through a tangled web of ghost corporations and aliases.

Brilliant and meticulous, he'd been planning his coup-de-grace for years—honing his skills, as it were. The cops had no idea how many kills he'd made, were too stupid to put the fragmented pieces together. And now, the time had come for the grand finale. He couldn't wait to show the snotty cow who was boss. He hoped she had a strong constitution. He intended to stretch the fun out for days.

Arriving at his destination with a hard-on, he opened the trunk and slung the hundred pounds of dead weight over his shoulder. Carrying it about fifteen feet from the gravel road, he dumped it, distorted face up. With a box cutter, he sliced the electrical ties from her bruised and bleeding wrists and sawed off hunks of her once-silken hair. These he spread them over and around the body. Of course, he kept one sweat matted tress for his collection.

Last but far from least, he opened her legs in a most undignified manner.

Stepping back, he perused the fruits of his labor, cursing himself for not having another roll of film. The effect was masterful, exquisite to the point of rendering a camera superfluous. The abused, mutilated body would forever hold a place of honor in his mind's eye.

Nonetheless, he made a mental note to have extra film on hand for next time...

Chapter 9

"It was like time stood still, Gi. It sounds cliche, but, we *were* the only two people in the world.

His lips. His eyes. His *kiss*—Oh my god, his kiss. It was breathtaking, I tell you. If I'd died from lack of oxygen, I'd have died happy."

Taking a breather after scouring Neiman-Marcus, Lulu Lemon and Victoria's Secrets, the experienced power shoppers re-energized for their second offensive. Sucking back fruit smoothies, they got in a little girl talk before tackling H&M's and Macy's. Without a scintilla of guilt, Zoey indulged her passion for french fries. Snagging one with the tips of two dainty fingers, she delivered it to her watering mouth with one fluid, practiced motion. Between fries, she filled Gianna in on her scalding encounter with Ash Harrington the night before.

"It sounds crazy, but it felt natural, almost familiar, as if it was meant to be. The electricity between us set off sparks the size of meteors."

She held back the crazier stuff. Like how their minds melded and their souls enmeshed, baring themselves without shame for the other to peruse.

Like how he'd felt her pain, intuited her anguish, and fed off her raw desire – as she'd done his.

Like how each became a part of other, and how nothing else existed.

That is, until the police burst in, guns drawn, trigger fingers twitching. Apparently, it's their duty to respond to any alarm, even those reported as false. When they arrive to find the establishment's door hanging ajar, they can become a tad aggressive.

Flashlight beams arced and probed until they honed in on what must have looked like two huddled intruders. Blinded, she and Ash squinted into the light, unable to see the muzzles aimed at their chests. She panted as much from the remnants of her star-spangled orgasm as she did from shock at the armed incursion.

"Police! Put your hands where we can see them! *Do it now!*"

To say the mood was ruined would understate the reality. Their hands flew up so fast, evidence of their carnal activity still shimmered in Ash's palm. He explained the misunderstanding with an embarrassed chuckle. When given the okay, he wiped his hand on his windbreaker then reached into the pocket for identification.

In so doing, he stepped away from her.

The first step could be explained away. The second could not. For some inexplicable reason, the man who'd enquired as to the moisture level of her 'cunt' seemed relieved at the intrusion.

Hmmm...

Using all five fingers, Zoey stuffed a ridiculous amount of greasy fries into her mouth. Chomping them into submission, she thrust the salt and gravy stained container at Gianna. Based on the look of horror she received in reply, an onlooker might suspect she'd offered her cyanide. Shrugging, she shoved her roommate's rebuffed portion into her mouth, as well. When she was able to speak, she hid her distress with humor.

"It was a real gong show, Gi. The only one who wasn't

there was you!"

She chuckled along with Gianna, but the smile didn't touch her eyes. She recalled how Ash hesitated when he'd first taken her into his arms. Could the momentary flash of anger she'd glimpsed in his eyes have been real, not imagined as she'd believed? Oddly, it was his very desire for her that seemed to enrage him. There'd been no mistaking the rigid outline of his passion. It had throbbed against her, impossible to ignore.

Zoey gnawed on the dichotomy and her lower lip before deciding to stop obsessing and let the man's kiss speak for itself. And, oh, my, that kiss had spoken volumes. Well worth the six months of longing that preceded it, she was already jonesing for a second close encounter with the addictive lips of Mr. Ash Harrington.

Preferably without police intervention this time...

Slurping the last of their smoothies, the long time friends rose as one. Gianna grabbed her two shopping bags, having all the luck thus far. The fire-engine red push-up bra and panty set in the Victoria's Secret bag turned Zoey's cheeks much the same color. As did the little—*very little*—black dress in the Neiman-Marcus bag. Gi, however, was a proud, cleavage baring proponent of the 'If Ya Got It, Flaunt It' movement.

She herself was more of a cotton sports bra and denims kind of girl. Flat as a board in her competitive days, her breasts had grown so large since that she preferred downplaying them to flaunting them. Pointing to the shopping bags, Zoey attempted to pry a little information from her newly-secretive best friend.

"Soo...where's the new man taking you in such a sexy

outfit, Geeg?"

When Gianna's eyes began to dance and her lips to part, Zoey was sure she was about to spill the beans. Instead...

BRRRING!

Strains of Beyonce's *Put a Ring On It* shattered the moment. Gi whipped out her phone faster than a cowboy whipped out his six-shooter at ten paces.

"Well, hello there, you!"

Whoever 'you' was caused every inch of Gianna's exposed skin to flush crimson. With a surreptitious glance in Zoey's direction, she veered off to the left, making sure she was out of earshot before continuing the conversation.

Flabbergasted, Zoey waited, wondered, and worried. *What in the world was going on?* She'd known Gianna for a dozen years. She'd never acted this way before. The dread that had gripped her earlier took hold once again, tighter this time. The hair on the back of her neck stood up, her skin crawled. Something was very, *very* wrong. Zoey didn't know what it was, but her intuition screamed for her to find out.

About ready to march over and demand Gianna come clean, her own phone pinged. She found it vibrating in the corner of her cross-shoulder satchel. Guiding it out, she double-tapped and gasped in surprise. It wasn't her ever-absent mother calling, something she'd promised to do days ago as she was gallivanting somewhere between the south of France and the Italian Riviera. No, the incoming text was from A. Harrington. Zoey's center of gravity shifted a foot due south. Already slick, the lips of her sex pressed against the confines of her little cotton panties.

That is, until she read the content of his missive. Around her, Zoey's world swirled out of focus, fifty shades of stomach

FALLEN

churning gray...

Chapter 10

A. Harrington: *I don't know what came over me last night. I wasn't myself. Please forgive me. It won't happen again.*

Ash dropped the phone as if it were diseased.

Like me...

A quick glance in the bathroom mirror told him what he already knew. He looked like a sack of shit. He felt like one, too. With the first photo shoot for his new cologne, *Harrington Gold*, scheduled for that afternoon, Ash knew what he needed to do. He needed to pull a fucking miracle out of his ass!

Barring that, his haggard appearance did not bode well for the future of his signature scent. Sure, he could deal with the dark overgrowth of two day old stubble. He could even plaster a 'come hither' smirk over the prevailing scowl of disgust. But, the dark circles under his eyes would require the impossible: a week's worth of uninterrupted sleep and an extended vacay.

One thing was certain, Versace's make-up artists would earn their pay this day.

Stepping into the shower, near-scalding water cascaded over his head and down his back. Full blast and needle sharp, his blood surged to the surface in a feeble attempt to mitigate the onslaught. Sucking in his breath, Ash stood his ground, accepting the punishing deluge as his due.

Not only hadn't he slept, he hadn't eaten – unless beer was a food group. Even his plan to work out the night before had been shot to hell the second he'd laid eyes on Zoey.

Zoey...

Shaking his head, something between a chuckle and a growl escaped his tight lips. She'd been quite the sight, screaming at the top of her lungs. *And, what a set of lungs they were!*

He tried to tell himself that he'd gathered her into his arms for the altruistic purpose of comforting her. And, perhaps he had. At first. Whatever his initial intent, it had little bearing on the outcome. Mother Nature was hellbent on having her way, as was the devil. Zoey tugged at his heart and whispered to his soul, her siren's song irresistible. There was no use in denying it.

The problem was what she did for his libido. On sight, the woman caused his dick to rise from the ashes like the proverbial phoenix. Last night, the temptation had been all-consuming, a runaway train hurtling downhill at top speed. He'd done his best to engage the emergency brake, had come *this*close to succeeding. In the end, however, even that desperate measure failed.

Months of self-discipline had fallen to the wayside in a single blink of her beautiful eyes.

Ash washed his hair, face, and armpits. Squeezing his eyes shut, he avoided the sting of shampoo while attempting to intercept the direction of his thoughts – and his now-twerking cock. Neither was possible. Far from banishing Zoey from his mind, she was his sole focus. There was no controlling his body's natural reaction.

Oh, how her eyes had sparkled up at him, a shade of green that defied description. Deep within them, he'd glimpsed joy and passion, but, also dark stains of fear and sadness. He wondered at their genesis, could almost feel her pain. Her lips on his were the perfect fit, their rhythm somehow familiar. He could have kissed her forever. In hindsight, he should have.

Cunth. Cunth dwenth, thir...

He couldn't lie, the words both nauseated and thrilled him. Shuddering, he grabbed for the soap and bent to lather his tree-trunk legs—his tree-trunk dick making the journey all the more difficult. Thank god the boys in blue arrived before things had progressed – *or regressed* – much further. Who knows what might have transpired. Mercedes was right, he *was* the sexual version of Jekyll and Hyde. Without an erection, he was just your average guy who's carnal desires fell well within the boundaries of social acceptability. The problem arose in tandem with his penis. At full mast, he turned into something he didn't recognize and didn't understand – something Dominant, demanding, and according to his ex-wife – disgustingly deviant.

Until Zoey, he'd been able to control the devil within through a steady diet of guilt and abstinence.

Reaching his groin, he threw abstinence to the wind. *Fuck it!* He wasn't about to show up to the photo shoot looking like crap *and* hobbling on three legs. Encircling the base of his cock with one soapy hand, he leaned against the shower wall, conjured Zoey's face, and did what came naturally. This time, he vowed to keep it clean.

It began well...

In the missionary position, he holds her tenderly, their lips glued, their tongues grasping. He enters her inch by inch until the whole of him fills the whole of her. He pauses to give her time to acclimate to his considerable girth. They gaze into each other's eyes as he whispers sweet nothings into her ear.

She whimpers, trembles, sighs.

Blah, blah, fucking blah...

By the time the first gush of semen makes its way to the drain, she's gagged, blindfolded, and bound to the four corners of his bed...

Chapter 11

"Check."

The King, King, seven flop gave Ash a full house, sevens full of Kings. With the highs and lows of international competition to draw from, his heart rate doesn't even flutter at the fortuitous turn of cards. It was just him and 'Slick' Stan in the hand and the pot was already hefty. While it was possible that Stan was holding a King/seven in his hand, the odds were against it. On the other hand, Stan was known to play almost any two cards, often three-betting the worst of them pre-flop.

As he'd done with this hand...

Ash took his time, considering and reconsidering, calculating and recalculating, giving nothing away, taking nothing for granted. Out of position, he decided to slow play, checking his monster hand to the big raiser. Stan bet large, too large. It came across as a transparent attempt to scare him off the pot. Stan wasn't quite as slick as he liked to think.

Ash knit his brow and glanced again at his pocket cards, hoping to convey weakness. As always, he took his sweet time. The asshole to his left began fidgeting and cracking his knuckles. Again. Whereas poker relaxed him, this guy was twanging his last nerve.

"I call."

He prayed the nine on the turn was a brick, but decided it was time to act. The last thing he wanted was to give Slick Stan the opportunity to build a slick hand.

"Check."

When Stan bet even bigger this time, Ash made his move. After a bogus display of apprehension, he re-raised.

Stan insta-folded, a look of disgust on his face.

"You're a shifty son of a bitch, Harrington. You're lucky I like you, have more money than god and can't play poker worth a shit!"

Except for the man on his left who'd stopped assaulting his knuckles long enough to check his watch, the table erupted in laughter. Ash chuckled along with his old pals, using both arms to rake in yet another pot courtesy of Stanwick Chase. Yeah, *that* Stanwick Chase. Stacking the impressive pile of chips, his mind made a beeline to its favorite subject.

Zoey...

His phone had been vibrating in its holster since he'd apologized for his beastly behavior hours before. He'd read her first message, none since. The one was enough.

But...I want it to happen again! I don't understand. Did I do something wrong?

There were now three unread and four unanswered messages from the woman he wanted with the whole of his being. The woman he was drawn to like a magnet, yet, could never have. The hurt in her words caused his heart to contract until his chest hurt. It wasn't her. She couldn't do anything 'wrong' if she tried. It was him that was wrong – from the inside out. There was no fix, no antidote. Which is why he would not, *could* not, relent.

For her sake...

At least the shoot for *Harrington Gold* had gone better than he'd anticipated. The set was dark, relegating his baggage-laden eyes and tight lips to moot points. He wasn't much more than a silhouette, a manly-smelling mystery shrouded in fog and swooning females. Or, such was the 'vision' explained to him by Will Waters, set director and photographer extraordinaire.

"Can you see it, Mr. Harrington? It's subliminal perfection, is it not?"

The frenetic man had clenched his hand just a fraction too tight and pumped it just a fraction too long. The prolonged contact caused a bad vibe to travel up his arm and settle in the pit of his stomach. It didn't help when terms such as 'world famous', 'illustrious', and 'brilliant' were bandied about in his honor. A pretentious smile was plastered on his face, stone-cold arrogance glinted in his eyes. Clearly, the guy wallowed in his own press.

Nothing unusual there...

His clothes were high end and custom tailored, yet as rumpled as pajamas. Ash wouldn't have been surprised to learn they'd been donned the previous day. His hands presented another striking contrast. While the palms were calloused, the nails were filed into perfect semi-circles and sparkled under layers of clear polish. He looked around Ash's age, but obvious signs of plastic surgery made it difficult to tell. His eyelids were pulled so tight, he barely blinked.

Sooo...nothing unusual there, either...

Ash had dismissed the ominous feeling as a by-product of his black mood exacerbated by his displeasure to find a new photographer. As timing would have it, Cassandra Taves was in Milan for Fashion Week. She'd done all the shoots for the first scent and he'd grown comfortable in front of her camera. By way of silent apology to the man he'd so savagely assessed, he threw himself into the shoot with more gusto than he felt. By the time it wrapped to rave reviews and an hour ahead of schedule, he'd invited Will Waters to the weekly Texas Hold'em game, as well.

It was a mistake he regretted. As it turned out, his initial assessment of Will Waters was spot on—the guy was just plain weird. Ping-ponging from chatty and inquisitive to distracted and distant, the one constant was his crackling knuckles. He also seemed very interested in the history of the NGTC. Not the present. Not the future. Just the history.

Like he said: weird.

If he couldn't put a finger on exactly why the guy pissed him off, it didn't negate the fact that he did. Where other's might find him charming, he found him manipulative. Where others might think him good looking, he saw a facade. Even Percy O'Malley seemed taken with the man. The police Chief, otherwise known as Percy 'The Nose', was almost as good at nailing bad guys as he was poker pots. He didn't get his nickname by tiptoeing softly through the tulips, either. It was said he could smell bullshit from a mile away. Yet, here he was, listening to this joker's grandiose stories and laughing at his old, worn out jokes.

When the photographer pushed himself away from the table and announced his early departure, Ash felt an undeniable rush of relief.

"Well, boys, I'm afraid I must reckon my losses and be off. Wouldn't want to keep the girlfriend waiting. You know how women are."

Winking and guffawing at his own sexist pronouncement, he cashed in what was left of his chips and left. Happy to be rid of him, Ash exhaled for what seemed like the first time all day. Under his breath, he wished the insufferable man's girlfriend the best of luck.

It struck him as he was anteing up for the next hand.

Girlfriend?

He was sure that at some point during the shoot, the narcissistic Mr. Waters had mentioned a wife. A 'hot' wife and a kid, in fact. Peeking at his hole cards, Ash mucked the Jack/six offsuit without engaging a brain cell and sighed. That the pompous ass was also a cheater should come as no surprise.

Nothing unusual there, right?

Wrong!

This time, Ash went with his gut and his morals. He looked forward to never seeing the 'illustrious, world-famous' creep again...

Chapter 12

Zoey was sick and tired of tossing and turning. Sitting up in frustration, she one-clicked the lamp on her bedside table and twirled her hair. Reaching for her phone, she double tapped, recoiling against the sudden glare. Her eyeballs, affronted by the onslaught, burned in their sockets. Her temples thumped like tom-toms.

Three-forty-seven and all was not well...

Scowling at the digits as though Father Time was pulling a dirty trick on her, she swung her legs over the side of the bed and shivered. The thin cotton nightie offered little by way of warmth. Huddling in the meager circle of lamplight, she pulled still-warm blankets around her quavering shoulders and across her goose-bumped thighs.

The chill remained.

As did the bile in her throat and the sick feeling in her gut. As far as sleep was concerned, it would have to wait until tomorrow. Or, perhaps, the day after. With one hand, she knotted and unknotted a wayward curl. Her decade-old habit didn't have the calming effect it usually did.

Damn that man!

At the thought of Ash Harrington and his cavalier dismissal of her, Zoey's jaw clenched, teeth gnashing. The pounding in her head ratcheted up from excruciating to damn near unbearable. Revelling in the pain, it was the only thing that kept her from sobbing. She'd done more than enough of that. Just ask her eyeballs.

I don't know what came over me last night. I wasn't myself. Please forgive me. It won't happen again.

Damn right it won't happen again. Since being blown off with the callous, nineteen word text, she'd buffeted between shock, despair, and anger. Each emotion came replete with its own flood of bitter tears. Reading his words that first time, her knees had actually buckled. Only the idea that she might faint in the middle of a crowded mall had kept her upright. She remembered her lips moving in Gianna's general direction, but words eluded her. Nonetheless, Gi was at her side in a heartbeat, concern etched into her features. If Zoey was half as pale as she felt, she'd have frightened ghosts.

Without a word, her best friend threw a supportive arm around her and helped her out to the car, H&M's and Macy's forgotten. By the time she collapsed into the passenger seat, the ringing in her ears had subsided enough to answer the question burning in Gianna's wide eyes. It was embarrassing to think that less than an hour earlier, she'd been singing Ash's praises, giddy at the thought of seeing him again and fantasizing about where their relationship might go.

What a difference a text made.

Thank god she'd held back the 'crazier' stuff'. Apparently, all that mind melding and soul meshing was a fat load of hooey. The only crazy was her. With grease and stomach acids burbling in her gut, she'd explained her Scarlett O'Hara worthy 'spell'.

"He's not interested in me, Geeg. No reason given. Just a nice polite fuck off, that's it. I have it in writing..."

Gianna's reaction was immediate, and passionate.

"Il bastardo!"

When she got riled, her Sicilian blood boiled. At five foot nothing and ninety pounds, she possessed the vernacular of a Mafia capo.

"Che cazza! I'd love to get my hands on the good for nothing son of a bitch! Strongo vaffanculo!"

With her crude suggestion that Ash go fuck himself, Gi reached across the console and pulled Zoey into a mama bear hug. With her face smushed against her friend's bony clavicle, the corners of her lips twitched upwards into a smile. How could they not? She hugged Gianna hard. She was the most loyal – and hilarious – friend a girl could ever have.

Shivering on the edge on her bed, she smiled again at the memory. As if on cue, the WD-40 resistant hinges on the front door squealed, more jarring than any doorbell. Zoey checked the time. It was awfully late, even for her impetuous roommate. Lifting the corner of the blind, tail lights flashed at the corner as a dark, four-door sedan turned left and disappeared. The bastard didn't even walk her to the door. She couldn't help but sneer at the sparkling hubcaps, adding vanity to an already extensive list of grievances against a man she'd never met and who's name she didn't know.

Zoey debated pulling a robe on and going to greet her closed-mouthed roomie. Before this new guy, there'd have been no hesitation. Before this new guy, nothing was off limits, there was no such thing as too much information. More often than not, they'd wind up in hysterics at Gianna's rapid-fire English/Italian descriptions of her date's shortcomings. Or long comings, as the case may be.

Ahem...

But, with Mr. Mysterio in the picture, there was nothing to discuss and even less to laugh about. Recalling the uncomfortable silences of late, she decided against it. Instead, she'd take one last stab at some shut eye. Work was just a few short hours away.

Work!

The thought of seeing Ash – or not seeing Ash—caused every muscle in her body to constrict, starting with her anus and ending with her heart. Stuck somewhere between despair and anger, confusion reigned supreme. Sighing, she slipped into bed and pulled the covers up to her nose. She was surprised when there was a soft knock at her door.

"Mio cara? Are you awake? I need to speak with you."

"At four thirty in the morning? But, of course I'm awake, darling. Come in..."

Chapter 13

Zoey decided the best way to end a disastrous day was with a cringe-worthy dose of humiliation. With her eyeballs bleeding into her throbbing skull, she circled the block three times before backing the little Acura into a parking spot.

She adored the sleek silver vehicle, given to her by her father three years earlier. On warm days, she'd swear she could still smell his aftershave. It was beyond devastating, watching the cancer take him. But, even as he withered away, he was teaching her invaluable life lessons about courage and grace under fire. He'd always been there for her, making up for an aloof, disinterested mother. She'd been honored to return the favor. It had nothing to do with duty and everything to do with love. If only she could have done more than just hold his hand and adjust his pillows. Between her dad and Hal, she was grateful to have had two such strong and honorable men in her life.

If she were going to tell anyone about Billy Pickton, it would have been dad. That door slammed shut the day he was diagnosed with Stage Four bone cancer that had metastasized to his lungs. Doctor Karvales hadn't looked him in the eye when he shook his hand and advised him to put his affairs in order. Four months later he was dead.

Parked in front of Ash's loft, she held firm to the leather-bound steering wheel. With a sigh, she banged her head against her white knuckles, trying to knock some sense into herself.

Thud!

Go home, you fucking martyr.

Thump!

Haven't you suffered enough for one day?

Whack!

Apparently not.

She shouldn't be here, she knew that. She knew before she shifted into drive and barreled through rush hour traffic to get here. Dad would advise against it, but he wasn't here. Her last ounce of common sense had evaporated at precisely ten minutes past three that afternoon. It took until that late hour to realize that the mighty 'Oak' Harrington – who's tongue was down her throat and who's fingers were rubbing her snatch just two nights previous—didn't have the gonads to face her. At ten minutes past three, confusion and fatigue turned into clarity and unabashed outrage.

Hell hath no fury like a woman scorned, asshole.

The bulk of her annoyance was self-directed, but she wasn't about to tell him that. He didn't need to know that *she* was the real asshole. She should have known better than to trust her instincts after Billy Pickton. For the first time in ten years she's attracted to a man and he turns out to be a heartless prick.

Gee, go figure...

Zoey shuddered, wishing she could delete the quartet of whining, snivelling – and unanswered—messages she left on his voice mail. In lieu of that, she was bound and determined to wrestle back some small shred of dignity.

Bravado bolstered, she turned off the engine and exited the car before her better judgement chimed in. It might remind her that wrestling anything away from a two-time Olympic gold medal wrestler might be a feat best performed after a good night's sleep and a heap load of careful consideration. Nonetheless, she was here, and, as such, the time was ripe. She'd been the timid one all her life. That changed today.

As determined as she was, her body was slow to cooperate. Her feet felt like lead as she dragged them – along with her sorry ass – to the building's front entrance. Her hand cramped as she swung open the heavy glass door. Her eyes blurred as she perused the short menu at the security booth. Thankfully, the instructions were simple enough: Press One for Bungalow, Two for Loft. Even in her altered state, she managed to press the right button. Twirling a stray lock of hair, she held her breath and waited. It rang three an a half times, clicked, then nothing.

He wasn't home.

Zoey exhaled, more relieved than she cared to admit. And yet, the silence was palpable, as though the line was left open. Shivering, she could almost feel his eyes on her, one scarred eyebrow raised in annoyance. Thinking of his many scars, her heart fluttered. She adored them, the jagged one on his lip in particular. She'd love to run her tongue across it, then smother it with kisses.

What the fuck was she talking about?

"Hello? Is someone there?"

More silence. She must have been imagining things. He wasn't there, it was just that simple. Either that, or...

"It's Zoey. Are you there, Ash?"

"I'm here, Zoey. The question is, what are you doing here?"

Now, it was her turn to pause. *What was she doing there?* Just the sound of his voice calmed her. There was no rhyme or reason for the effect he continued to have on her.

Common sense and the heart had little, if anything, to do with each other, she was learning that the hard way. Exhaling so hard her cheeks puffed out, she told him the truth.

"I'm not sure. I'm tired, I'm sad, and I'm super pissed off. I didn't know what else to do. The other night, I felt..."

Thinking better of finishing that remark, she decided instead to make a long story short.

"I just need some closure. Then I'll go, I promise."

With nothing left to say, she waited. She wouldn't beg. She was about to leave when the interior door grated open before her. His voice trailed her into the building, a mixture of irritation and resignation.

"You deserve at least that, Zoey. Come up..."

Chapter 14

With both of her wrists secured, he stretched her arms as far above her head as they would go. For good measure, he pressed them an inch further. Holding them there with one hand, he groped under her sweater for her tits with the other. Pushing the cotton bra aside, he mauled the flesh and flicked at the rock hard nipples. His thigh was shoved between the two of hers, pushed up as high as it could go. Abrading the soft cotton of her panties with the rough denim of his jeans, he held her immobile against the door she should never have passed through.

God, she was beautiful...

He'd sworn to curb his impulses before he buzzed her in, and true to form, he'd failed. *Ah, well.* Around Zoey, self-control was just two words separated by a hyphen. She took his breath away, along with his good and common sense. With innate proficiency, the woman pushed buttons he didn't know existed – most notably the one that caused his dick to rise like a fucking beacon, then to drool like Pavlov's dog post dinner bell.

Today, she'd come too close and pushed too far. Now, he was pushing back. He squeezed her wrists until she whimpered.

"*This* is why I have to stay the fuck away from you, *okay?* Do you get it yet? You should have gotten it the other night and stayed the fuck away."

To ensure he had her full attention, he caught one nipple between his middle and index fingers and squeezed until she gasped into his face. Watching her pupils dilate as she assimilated the sensation was a sight too breathtaking for words.

Fuck, he wanted to kiss her...

"There's something wrong with me. Ask Mercedes, she'll be only too happy to fill you in on the gory details. The point is, the only way I seem able to control myself around you is to not be around you. As you can see, your coming here makes that difficult. You're too sweet, too...clean...for me to corrupt, Zoey. You deserve better. Now, get the hell out of here before I strip you naked and have my perverted way with you."

He did not loosen his grip. Instead, he squeezed harder, waiting for her outraged demand that he unhand her, followed by a well deserved go-fuck-yourself as she stormed out the door. When she moaned, arched into the pressure at her nipple, and ground against his thigh—it was his turn to gasp.

"I deserve better? Better than what my heart calls for? I may not be experienced, but I'm not as sweet, nor as clean, as you contend. What I 'got' the other night is that I want more. So, if there's something wrong with you, then there's something wrong with me, as well. I don't know what bullshit your ex tried to feed you, but it's her problem, not yours. Any woman who tells you they don't want their man to push their limits a little in the bedroom is lying."

Was she right? Was it possible that his needs had been hobbled by a woman terrified of her own? After being whipped for years, he'd swallowed Mercedes ceaseless assertions that he was a monster hook, line, and sinker. Married too young and too long, he was far from experienced himself. A vision of his ex-wife flashed in his mind. Her arms were bound, her nipples clamped. Screaming like a banshee, her entire body was vibrating from an extended orgasm.

Another extended orgasm. In hindsight, her accusations that he was a sick puppy in desperate need of help didn't come until *after* she did—multiple times.

The idea that he might embrace his true nature instead of running from it had never occurred to him. It was a thrilling hypothesis indeed, almost as thrilling as the woman who proposed it. He would ponder it further and at length. Later. At the moment, that same woman was humping his leg like a bitch in heat, her eyes rolled back in her head.

A wet spot formed on his thigh, dark and glutinous. His cock surged at the sight, as did his imagination. On testosterone overload, he inhaled her pheromones and growled. Zoey was to his libido what a match was to gasoline. A second wet spot appeared on the front of his jeans. It marked the exact location where the distended tip of his cock wept with impatience.

"Zoey..."

If she didn't leave now, he couldn't be responsible for his actions. Her eyes snapped into his, smoky green with a glaze of unabashed lust. Adrift in their depths, he encountered a vulnerability that touched his heart. The lesions of pain and fear he'd discovered two nights before hung in the background, ever present. Whatever altruistic rubbish he was about to spout fell to the wayside. Overcome with a fierce desire to protect her, he could only wonder at the tragedies she'd suffered.

Jesus, he was falling in love...

As if she'd read his mind, Zoey's lips parted to meet his. His tongue made a beeline for hers, only to find it already in his mouth, searching for his. Their breath came in snorts and gasps, reminiscent of rutting bulls. Her eyes fluttered but remained open, offering direct access to her soul. Above her head, she grasped his thumb with both hands as her hips pumped against his thigh. There was no mistaking her body's gyrations. The rhythm was as old as time.

Their lips came apart a split second before one devoured the other. Her chest heaved, heart pumping triple-time into the palm of his roaming hand. If the four words she whispered were barely audible, their impact was nonetheless staggering.

"Please, Ash, corrupt me..."

Gobsmacked, his grip on her wrists loosened. Taking advantage of the momentary lapse, Zoey wriggled free, swung a graceful leg over his thigh, and with a contented sigh—dropped to her knees at his feet.

If there were a moon, he'd be howling at it...

Chapter 15

Sweeping away her fumbling hands, he undid his belt with a jerk and a pull. She'd grappled with it long enough.

By now, his dick was hammering in protest of its tight confines. In phallic Morse code, it demanded freedom. Yet, based on what he'd seen so far, the odds of that happening any time soon looked grim. If Zoey was as proficient with buttons and zippers as she was with belts, they could be here all week. That is, if she stuck around that long. She may talk tough, but the truth was, she was naive as hell. She had no conception of what she was getting herself into or what he was capable of.

She couldn't even manage his belt, for christ sake.

But, my, oh my, she looked delectable at his feet, as though she was born to kneel there. Brows furrowed, she gnawed her bottom lip as she concentrated on the task at hand. When she gazed up at him with despair and exasperation in her big green eyes, his heart melted. Smiling, he reached down to stroke her cheek and push a mop of unruly ringlets from her flushed face.

The better to see you, my dear...

As natural as she seemed on her knees, he'd put money down that she'd never fellated a man in her life. On the one hand, he wondered why. On the other, he relished the thought of guiding her through the nuances. But, first thing's first. At the moment, he was deeply concerned for the welfare of his tortured dick. Instead of tearing off his jeans and unfurling the painfully swollen appendage, he put his hands on his hips and channeled Job. Gnashing his teeth, he did a poor imitation of the patient man.

"Keep trying babygirl. It just takes practice. I'm a patient man."

Her smile was radiant. If it wasn't for the concrete barrier in his pants, he'd bend down to nuzzle the adorable dimple at the corner of her mouth. After just a few more tries, she popped the button and was making significant progress on the zipper. His patience expired the moment the last teeth separated.

"Good girl!"

She delighted in the praise. Placing her hands in her lap and squaring her shoulders, a shit-eating grin of accomplishment spread across her face. She wasn't getting off that easy, however. There was plenty of work yet to be done. One didn't start a blaze and then leave it to burn unattended. It was time for her to put her money, or in this case – his cock – where her mouth was. His balls roiled, hard at work preparing the huge load of semen that, very soon, would be coating her face and dripping off her tits. At least, that was the plan. The inherent risks were obvious.

For one, the door was directly behind her. She could be on the other side of it racing for her car in the blink of an eye. While he loathed the idea of losing her, the idea of falling irrevocably in love and *then* losing her was far worse. Life may not come with guarantees, but there was nothing wrong with covering a few bases.

Today, Zoey would get a taste of the real Ash Harrington.

Chuckling at the double entendre, he pushed his jeans, together with his briefs, to his ankles. Stepping out of them, his cock sprung free, a thick eight inches of purple veins and mushroom head. Slathered with pre-cum, it bounced like a springboard not two inches from Zoey's shocked face. Her eyes widened to the size of saucers.

"Don't just sit there gawking, girl. Say hello."

Not waiting for his words to sink in, he gripped the base and wiped a pearlescent glob of pre-cum across her cheek. Zoey's mouth fell open as it congealed and began to slide down her face.

"That's right, baby. Open wide."

Scooping up a second globule with two fingers, he applied it like gloss to her parted lips. Her throat clicked as she swallowed hard. Yet, it wasn't long until the tip of her tongue poked out to taste his seed for the first time. A hesitant sampling led to her sucking her lips clean with a ravenous moan. The vision warmed the cockles of his heart.

Not to mention his actual cockle...

Chapter 16

Please, Ash, corrupt me...

The words were out of her mouth before she could think to stop them. Thank god. Head spinning, Zoey sniffed at the bloated, drooling phallus that joggled inches from here face. Faint from euphoria and fueled by lust, she savored the man, the moment, and, most of all—the pungent bouquet of his scrotum.

If someone had told her an hour earlier that she'd be on all fours inhaling Ash Harrington's ball sweat, she'd have suggested they undergo an emergency psych evaluation. And, yet, here she was doing exactly that and loving every libidinous moment of it. Even before her knees touched the ground, she knew it was where she belonged. Kneeling at Ash's feet felt as natural as breathing, instant panacea for her soul. Just like that, she'd found her safe haven.

With that said, it was also her first up close and personal encounter with the male sex organ.

He'd given no warning before nonchalantly stripping off his skivvies. His cock burst forth with such ferocity, she'd squealed and ducked, circumventing possible damage to her nose. Bobbing in front of her face, it didn't take long before she was utterly smitten.

The tip seemed huge, encompassing several shades of purple and leaking pre-cum in long shimmery threads. She needed only to stick out her tongue to catch one. The shaft reminded her of a gnarled tree trunk. The skin was stretched so tight, she could make out the intricate maze of veins just beneath the surface. Her nipples tingled in anticipation of running her tongue along it.

Yum...

But, it was his balls that fascinated her most. Not only were they huge and hairy, they...churned...causing her drenched pussy to spasm in unison. Her poor panties were so saturated, they drooped like a cheap diaper. Enthralled with the panoramic man-scape before her, she was stunned when a globule of pre-cum was smeared across her face. There'd been little time to react before a second was coating her lips.

Now, with her nose buried in his balls, she reached out to wrap her hand around the root as she'd watched him do.

"No hands! In fact, clasp them behind your back and keep them there. If you can't manage, I'll be happy to fetch some rope."

She barely had time to comply before Ash's thick fingers were combing through her hair. Helping himself to a handful, he jerked her head up until her lips were in direct alignment with his cock. Just in case she misinterpreted his meaning, he was good enough to clarify.

"Suck it."

And she did. Or, at least, she tried. She mouthed the slippery tip, no doubt thinking herself ever-so-risque. She was suckling at the oozing pee hole when she was unceremoniously wrenched away and shown the true meaning of his words. His free hand came out of nowhere to once again grasp the base of his now-quivering member. Pressing it to her lips, he tightened the grip on her hair. He held her head steady as slowly but surely, inch by inch, he fed his cock into her mouth.

Floating somewhere outside of her body, she watched her lips stretch to obscene proportions in order to accommodate the oversized head. He paused when she started to gag. Panicked, she struggled, unbinding her hands in order to press them against his thighs. It was no use. She wasn't going anywhere.

"Easy, babygirl. It's okay. You just need to relax your throat. Will you try?"

His voice washed over her, soothing and warm. She wasn't sure if the tears on her cheeks were due to the cock jammed down her throat or the sweet ache in her heart. When he reached down to massage her throat, she whimpered, more determined than ever to please him.

Breathing through her nose like an ornery bull, she followed his guidance. Soon, she'd swallowed him almost to the nuts, her nose buried in fragrant, if bristly, pubic hair. Inhaling deeply, she gurgled with pride. When the cock in her mouth surged in length, breadth, *and* girth, she was exhilarated despite her distended larynx.

He pumping into her, slowly at first, then faster and faster. Snot ran from her nose, tears from her eyes, and hot, sticky, desire from her pussy.

"Play with yourself, babygirl. I want to watch you come."

From her lofty position outside of her body, she watched herself bury a hand between her legs and begin to work her bulging clit. Sweaty and grunting, she hardly recognized herself. He sawed into her mouth again and again, saliva pouring from her lips to drip off his balls. When his entire body began to shudder, she was more than ready – she was right there with him.

The first spurt of hot jism shot down her throat just as the first wave of her own orgasm rocketed through her body. On instinct, she swallowed. Immersed in an ecstasy she'd never known, she guzzled down wave after wave of hot semen. She was unaware when it overflowed her mouth to pool between her legs.

Milking the last drops from his depleted balls, she collapsed to the floor, a heaving, twitching mass of wanton flesh. He lifted her as though she weighed nothing. Snuggled against his massive chest, she turned her face upward, too exhausted to open her eyes.

"I...I'm...You..."

Her lips felt swollen to twice their normal size while her brain felt diminished by that much or more. She might find the dichotomy amusing if she were able to concentrate on anything other than Ash.

"Shhh, baby, I know. I feel the same way."

His lips brushed her, ever-so-gently. Sighing, she was close to falling asleep in his arms. He carried her down the hallway in what she assumed was the direction of his bedroom. Kicking open the door, he crossed the threshold before nuzzling her ear. His voice was like velvet, deep and smooth. His words, however, sent shivers down her spine.

"And, don't think there won't be consequences for using your hands, my dear..."

Chapter 17

He slid the metal plate back into place and climbed down from the table, placing the shoebox upon it. Snapping his knuckles in anticipation, he rifled through it until he found the tattered photo. It was never far from the top. Taking a seat in the only available chair, he sneered at the faded image. Aroused and enraged in equal parts, he spoke to the girl as if she were sitting across from him. His tone was conversational. After all, there was no arguing with facts.

"You're a worthless whore. Just like the rest of them."

The beaming young girl in the red gown represented his most epic failure. On the other hand, it was thrilling to think about the sadistic games he'd fashioned to rectify that faux pas. They said that revenge was a dish best served cold. He said bullshit. Revenge was a dish best served with a nice tight garrotte and a rock-hard dick.

Gentle as a lover, he traced her entire silhouette with his forefinger. When he got to her throat, he switched from soft pad to sharp nail – sawing it back and forth from ear to ear. The marks it left joined countless others. His co-conspirator did a happy dance in his pants. Patting his tumescent partner in crime, he chuckled. As usual, they were in complete agreement.

"I know. I can't wait either."

He rummaged through the shoe box for the lock of hair. Removing the thick curl from its hermetically sealed capsule, he held it against his face and inhaled until his lungs were near to bursting. To his olfactory system, it reeked of moldy mothballs. To his temporal lobe, it smelled of rosebuds and missed opportunity. She was his first. She was also the only one that got away.

Ever.

From the small table in the corner, he perused his playground. He'd put a lot of time and effort into the oversized storage unit, and had to admit it was spectacular. Partitioned into three rooms, the front looked like any other storage unit anywhere. Packed to the rafters with boxes and old furniture, there was still plenty of room to pull his car in off the street. The second room served as his dark room. He was sitting in the third. It was his favorite. He liked to call it the games room.

The sound proofing panels were the best on the market. High pitched screams and hysterical sobbing were both one hundred per cent stifled. He knew. He'd tested the theory and was terribly impressed with the results.

Like they said in real estate, location was everything. Off the beaten track, there was nothing but open fields and train tracks in back. For years, he'd made a habit of coming and going at all hours. It wouldn't do to raise eyebrows at three in the morning when a naked, duct-taped girl might be wriggling in the trunk. With a hobby such as his, one couldn't be too careful.

In the end, his vigilance was for naught. Other than his double unit there were four other singles. Rented since the dawn of time, none of them saw much traffic. Even better, the security cameras were there for show, having never been activated. He learned this salient detail from Darryl, the dumb-as-a-stump manager. Next to picking at his acne, girl on girl on girl porn, and gin fucking rummy – Darryl's favorite pastime was spilling his guts to anyone that would listen.

"Boss says they're too 'spensive.   It ain't like nuttin' exciting ever happens 'round here, anyhow. Yuk, yuk, yuk."

Yeah, nuttin'. Yuk, yuk, yuk...

Leaning back, he twirled the lock of hair and wondered if she ever thought of him. He'd never been sure of what she knew for a fact – and what she only suspected. He made a mental note to enquire at their impending reunion. The stars were aligned, not to mention he had an ace up his sleeve. Thinking of his annoying-as-fuck 'ace', he hoarked deep in his throat, a bad taste in his mouth. His dick shriveled to nothing in his pants. Burying his nose in the faded tresses, he pushed all negative thoughts from his head and concentrated on the pot of gold at the end of the bullshit.

He remembered the night it all begun. It had been magical.

He'd picked her up in his new car. The tricked out Mustang was a graduation gift from his broken parents. Although he'd requested a Porsche, the gesture spoke to the extent of their elation that he was leaving. Of course, the feeling was mutual.

The perfect gentleman, he'd gone to the door to fetch her. He'd never forget how his heart had raced at the sight of her. Hair color aside, she was the perfect naive Barbie to compliment his cunning Ken. After smiling at her inattentive mother and shaking the hand of her overbearing father, he fastened a corsage around her wrist. Made up of red and white rosebuds, it was adorned with sprigs of baby's breath and curls of white ribbon. The scent filled the foyer. Never without his camera, he'd asked her father to take a picture.

He didn't know that photo was to hold the place of honor

in his shoebox for a decade. After all, he'd planned obsessively for months, believing he'd left nothing to chance. It wasn't a simple coup by any stretch. A precious commodity, she was protected better than Fort Knox. She was three years younger than him, as well – scandalous in teenager terms. Whereas he was a graduating senior, football hero and prom king, she was a sweet, virginal freshman who just happened to represent the hopes and dreams of a nation. Like so many others, he'd watched her grow and develop until she was standing on the very pinnacle of super-stardom.

Unlike so many others, he didn't imagine her on a podium with the national anthem playing in the background. He imagined an event far more significant. She was to have the honor of being his first victim. Now, she would have the honor of being his last.

At least on this continent...

When he was done with her, there would be every reason to leave. He planned to uproot Irina and the brat and get the fuck out of Dodge. Perhaps to Zagreb, where they'd met. He'd been on a photo shoot in Croatia and had decided to extend his stay to explore the nooks and crannies of the city. Irina, along with her parents and seven siblings, lived in the most impoverished of these.

Young, dumb, and desperate for a better life, instinct told him she'd make the perfect foil, behind which he could ply his sadistic trade with impunity. He imagined them joining their local church, pious and respected. He fixed her rotten teeth and resisted the urge to beat her, at least until they were out of the country. Then, with Irina's new and dazzling smile, he'd made her his wife. She couldn't speak a syllable of English.

Now, that's what he called happily ever after...

His revived dick demanded attention. Pulling the pudgy five and a half inches from his pants, he smirked at it. Their years of patience, practice and meticulous planning were about to pay off.

At last, they'd come full circle...

Chapter 18

A few steps from the gym, Zoey did her best to wipe the stupid grin off her face. The feat was more difficult than a backward stalder with a full twist. She was the cat, that, after an excess of sour milk, finally got the cream. A belly full, in fact. Thinking of her night with Ash, she purred with contentment. While she managed to not smack her lips, the stupid grin remained in tact.

Based on euphoria, she figured she could sleep when she was dead. Based on reality, it promised to be a long day. Her eyes burned. A porter could carry the dark, puffy bags beneath them. Her jaw ached, as did her throat every time she swallowed. Not surprising considering it was repeatedly violated with something the size of a cucumber. Last but not least, her knees stung, raw from carpet burn.

Still grinning, she straightened her shoulders and lifted her chin. Each grievance came with a satisfying dollop of pride. Last night, she'd been naughty. Very naughty. As naughty as any character in any book she'd ever read – and she'd read plenty. Flushing from head to toe, the muscles deep in her belly contracted. With one shuddering Kegel, her panties were damp. It was clear that she'd fight through a pack of thirsty vampires on a moonless night for the chance to do it again.

With Ash, naughty wasn't nice – it was orgasmic!

Speaking of Ash, they had a date planned for after work. He'd been inscrutable, saying only that he had something special planned. Even after she peppered him with questions, he refused to offer up a single clue. All she could do was wait and wonder.

"Until then, have a wonderful day, babygirl. Don't forget to think of me."

Yeah, like there was a snowball's chance in hell of that happening. Giddy with anticipation, the level of humidity in her underpants soared from damp to drenched. Incredulous at her body's organic reaction to the man, she shook her head.

Like she said: *Naughty!*

Taking a deep breath, she pushed open the front doors of the NGTC, her second home for a dozen years and counting. Familiarity enveloped her like a warm hug. With a seven hour training session underway, the gym was a beehive of high-flying activity. Eight ambitious athletes on four perilous pieces of apparatus were scrutinized from every angle by five hyper-critical coaches. She knew better than to call out or even to wave.

Describing the environment as a pressure cooker was putting it mildly. The laws of the jungle prevailed, survival of the fittest the name of the game. Tension and expectation hung heavy in the air, as did the pungent body odor associated with acute physical and mental exertion.

Carrie-Ann Douglas, the gum-snapping firecracker from Tallahassee, was marking out her floor routine to her new music.

Sasha Washington was on vault, her specialty. To watch her execute an Amanar was like watching poetry in motion. She was working on adding an extra half-twist, unthinkable in Zoey's day.

Tara Capers, also known as English Rose, was a visitor to the NGTC from across the pond. Here to have her skills assessed, it didn't look like she'd be sticking around long.

Already labeled a drama queen, she was living up to the moniker this morning. Standing on a balance beam, tears streamed down her cheeks. Nancy Ells, a two time Olympian turned beam coach scowled up at her, hands on hips.

"No! You cannot get down to chalk up. When you've stuck five in a row, you can chalk up before your next five. It's a basic flip-flop, Tara. Stop being ridiculous."

Zoey felt bad for the poor girl, but such was life in the jungle...

Cherish Harrington was working her reverse giant sequence on bars. Driven and talented, she reminded Zoey of her father. Minus the fifty-two inch chest and tree trunk legs, of course. Rubbing her bad shoulder, she grimaced. Even ten years after the injury, it twanged with each of Cherish's rotations.

Filling her lungs, she savored the acrid bouquet. It was an environment she'd thrived in. Until Billy. After Billy, it was an environment in which she could at least find sanctuary. Making her way down the long center corridor to the office, she couldn't help but think of Hal. As indomitable in death as he was in life, her old coach's energy permeated the twenty thousand square foot facility he'd built from the ground up.

She could almost hear his voice booming as he paced the same corridor. The walls would shake and the girls would quake as he stomped from one end to the other. Shoulders hunched, his bull-sized head would swivel non-stop, missing nothing. Seeing him approach, the hundred pound gymnasts would redouble their already Herculean efforts. Catching 'HAL' was not something anyone with half a brain cell wanted to experience twice. Yet, every last ounce of the enormous man was lovable. He gave his all to the girls he trained. They were his children.

In the small office, Zoey hung up her coat, fixed a pot of coffee, and assumed the position. Another day, another dollar. It took all of three minutes before she was checking the time and thinking of Ash.

When he'd carried her to his bedroom, she was hoping it was to make good on his threat to 'rip her clothes off and have his way with her'. Instead, he laid her ever-so-gently on his bed, then propped himself up on his elbow beside her. He brushed stray curls from her face with a tenderness that belied his bulk.

"You're beautiful, Zoey Benton. Inside and out."

Her throat closed, clogged with emotion. Thankfully, there was no need to respond. At his side, she was whole. A willing prisoner in the bottomless depths of his eyes, she didn't bother to wipe away the tears leaking from her own. Leaning over her, Ash used his tongue to eradicate them. Her ragged sigh came from the center of her being. She was fast falling in love with this thrilling dichotomy of a man. His words were as moving as the mind-bending orgasm she'd just experienced.

"I could get very used to gazing into those amazing eyes of yours, my darling."

As soft as a whisper, he traced her eyelids with his fingertip, then followed the same path with his lips. Feather kissing his way across her brow and down her nose, her lips were primed and parted by the time his arrived. When his mouth took hers at last, the kiss was not borne of carnal passion but of spiritual communion. It was glorious.

Fifteen minutes later, she was in her car heading home.

FALLEN

Not by choice...

Chapter 19

"Are you and Zoey dating, dad?"

The guileless question set Zoey's cheeks aflame. Finally, it was quitting time. Ash had just arrived to pick her up. Ogling him from beneath lowered lashes, she was grateful for her swollen lips. They made it impractical to let loose with a most unbecoming wolf whistle. With Cherish at her side, Zoey had a serious word with the brazen hussy within.

Down girl!

Still, there was no harm in looking. Dressed down, Ash wore a black T-shirt with the sleeves torn off. His chest and shoulders were impossibly broad, stippled with thick bands of muscle. With the smallest provocation, tendons rippled through them likes waves. His jeans were faded and holey, not to mention scrumptiously snug. The combination of his ass and those jeans ought to come with a warning label. Allowing the brazen hussy within just a moment's freedom, Zoey's eyes devoured his massive thighs before skimming over what lay between. Images from the previous evening leapt to mind.

Quickly moving on...

"Well, Daddy? Are you?"

Ash leaned down to kiss the top of his daughter's head. With one eyebrow cocked in her direction, he stalled, floundering for an answer. She grinned when he winked over Cherish's head, a devilish sparkle in his eye.

"Why don't you ask Zoey that question, monkey?"

"I already did. She said to ask you."

"Is that so?"

"Yes, that's so."

Watching father and daughter interact, her heart melted. The resemblance was strong, the love between them stronger.

"Well, when either of you figures it out, let me know, okay? If you ask my opinion, I think it'd be awesome!"

"I don't recall asking, Cher, but, I appreciate the input."

"You're welcome. Anytime."

Cherish's entire face crinkled, so wide was the smile she bestowed on her father. Ash ruffled her hair, then glanced out into the main gym.

"And, why aren't you doing your conditioning like everyone else, young lady?"

"I got permission to skip part of it. Zoey's agreed to teach me the Benton Twist, haven't you Zoey? I want it in my routine for Nationals. I know I can do it. Bars is my best event."

Cherish held up the notes she'd made over the past thirty-five minutes. They were based on Zoey's verbal dissection of her signature move and a slow motion video looping on *YouTube*.

"I want to try it for real tomorrow. You'll help me, right Zoey?"

"If Viktor says it's alright, I'd love to, hon."

The Benton Twist was still considered one of the most difficult bar dismounts to master. While many tried and failed, Cherish had a real shot at nailing it. Besides being blessed with her father's natural athletic ability, they shared a mile-wide stubborn streak. She wouldn't give up until she got it or died trying.

"Remember the secret I told you. After the second giant, hold on as long as you can before pulling your hip and shoulder hard right. You should go flying off that bar."

With a nod and a quick hug for both of them, Cherish zipped back to join the others for the end of conditioning. There wasn't a gymnast in the world that didn't interpret 'conditioning' as hell on earth. One grueling hour in duration, it followed a grueling hour of ballet and five grueling hours of apparatus work. At the door, she and Ash paused to observe.

Still in pairs, the octet of tough-as-nails teenagers went through a brutal circuit of strengthening exercises. Fifty basic pushups were followed by fifty basic situps. Twenty single-armed pushups were followed by three minutes of holding plank position with a coach pressing on their backs. By the time they got to ten leg lifts in straddle followed by ten leg lifts in pike followed by ten chin-ups?

Zoey was exhausted.

It boggled the mind to think this used to be her life. From the perspective of an ancient twenty-six year old, she was thankful that today—it was *them*, not her. She'd come to accept that her time had come and gone, leaving her on the sidelines. Billy Pickton aside, she was no different than so many other who *almost* made it, but didn't. Nonetheless, it was by far the greatest experience of her life. She may not have gone all the way, but the journey built character and instilled confidence.

In her proudly biased opinion, gymnastics was the greatest sport ever invented.

Buckled into Ash's SUV, she could no longer contain herself. She drank in the sexy, multifaceted man behind the wheel. Before he could get the key into the ignition, she was asking the burning question that had consumed her for most of the day.

"So, am I allowed to know where you're taking me yet?"

In lieu of an answer, Ash leaned across the console. Pulling her lower lip down with the pad of his thumb, he used that leverage to pull her closer – and kissed her. She was still moaning when he popped the glove compartment and withdrew a bandanna.

"Not quite yet, beautiful."

Flattening the bandanna on his thigh, he folded it like an accordion. It wasn't until he held it before her eyes that she understood. Her gasp was involuntary, as was the hot rush of moisture that radiated from the center of her being and wound up in the crotch of her already saturated panties.

"Do you trust me Zoey?"

Swallowing hard, she could only nod, unable to find her voice. In tacit surrender, she turned away from him, making it easier to tie the pseudo blindfold behind her head.

With one sharp tug, her world went black...

Chapter 20

"Hold on to that tree with both hands, my sweet. Make no mistake, if you let go, it will be my pleasure to begin again."

Legs straight and torso bent to ninety degrees at the hip, Zoey clasped her hands around the smooth bark and held on. Tight. Her sodden panties were no longer a concern, having been removed along with everything else. Naked as the jay birds twittering above, her breasts swayed beneath her and her bottom jutted out behind. After close – *very close* – inspection, Ash pronounced it the perfect target. Slick with perspiration and hornier than a toad, her breath hissed from her lungs in dread – and anticipation – of the first strike.

Don't think there won't be consequences for using your hands, my dear...

Ash Harrington was a man of his word. Blindfold in place, they'd driven for what seemed an eternity before finally turning onto a gravel road and pulling to a stop. With one hand on the wheel and one hand roaming her body, he'd worked her into a mindless, whimpering froth. She'd have writhed across the console and into his lap if she weren't virtually glued to the passenger seat.

When at last he turned off the vehicle and helped her out, the stench of the city was replaced with fresh air and honeysuckle. Birds sang. Leaves rustled. Stress melted away.

"It's beautiful, Ash."

"Wait, babygirl. There's more."

And, with those words, he removed the blindfold. Squinting against the light, her eyes took a few seconds to adjust. When they did, she gasped, overwhelmed to the point of tears.

In the middle of god knew where, the natural beauty was like chicken soup for her soul. Growing up, she'd rarely ventured outside of the gym, never mind outside of the city. Standing in a small clearing, they were surrounded on all sides by a virtual wall of trees. The setting sun sliced through their branches to carpet the landscape with ribbons of shimmering color. A butterfly came out of nowhere and hovered in front of her face. For a moment, it looked like it might land in her hair.

While the wonders of nature were wondrous indeed, it was the man-made accoutrements that left her weak in the knees. A blanket was spread under a tall poplar. Keeping it from blowing away was a large picnic basket, a bottle of wine, and a bouquet of hand-picked wildflowers. Whirling on Ash, she stared at him slack-jawed.

"Oh my god. How...*when* did you do this?"

"When I falling in love with you, that's when."

In complete shock, Zoey refused to believe her ears. *Did he just say what she thought he said?* Ash didn't give her the chance to think. Or ask. Or respond in kind. His eyes danced as he pressed a forefinger to her lips.

"Ssshhh..."

Taking her hand, he showed her around their private enclave. Strolling the perimeter, he pointed out the different trees. Maple, oak, birch, spruce. When they came upon a lone willow, he stopped.

"Please choose a switch, my dear, whichever one tickles your fancy. I can assure you, it won't be tickling that shapely ass of yours."

A what?

"A what?"

Ash took her by her upper arms and turned her to face him. His face was stern, in contrast to the upturned corners of his mouth and the twinkle in his eye.

"A switch. A smooth flexible branch. Otherwise known as a spanking utensil. Did you forget my promise, darling?"

Don't think there won't be consequences for using your hands, my dear...

She could actually feel the blood drain from her face. She'd never imagined.

"No. I...didn't forget, but..."

When he hugged her to him, the bulge in his pants was unmistakable. And enormous. Whatever she was about to add was forgotten.

"That's my girl!"

* * * * *

The first stroke set her left buttock on fire. If the birds were still chirping, she didn't hear them. Her mind was purged of any thoughts that didn't pertain directly to her left buttock. While she managed to keep her hands clasped, she jerked ramrod straight, instinctively pulling her burning butt out of the line of fire.

When the five-alarm inferno dissipated to a warm glow, she became aware of something else: the thrumming of her clit and the spatter of pussy juice running down her thigh. Suddenly, her face was burning hotter than her ass.

"Did you enjoy that, darling?"

She wanted to answer. Would have if she could have. But, before she could find words, the crunch of leaves marked his approach. His hands cupped her perspiring face, as gentle as the blow was harsh. Her vision cleared and his strong features came into focus. They were contorted with concern.

"Babygirl. The last thing in the world I want to do is hurt you. If you don't want to continue, all you need do is let go of the tree. I'll understand, believe me I will. I warned you that when I get aroused, the Dominant in me takes over. I can't say I'm sorry, but, when I'm with you? I'm aroused. It's as simple as that."

He paused to kiss her forehead, her eyelids, the tip of her nose. One hand left her face to reappear between her legs. It came away dripping, of course. When he chuckled, she squirmed under his knowing gaze. There was no disguising the obvious. When she was with Ash? She was aroused. It was as simple as that.

One at a time, Ash sucked his fingers clean as if they were ribs slathered in barbeque sauce. She was panting goggle-eyed by the time he licked the last of her from his lips and grinned. He looked like the fox who'd just unearthed the master key to the hen house.

"On the other hand, my lovely, if you'd like me to continue – please assume the position!"

Nine glorious strokes later, she was floating in sub-space and Ash was buried to the hilt inside her. It was embarrassing to think that she was still a virgin at the age of twenty-six. At least, she was a virgin to the best of her knowledge. There was a moment of panic, a flashback just when he began to enter her, but it was obliterated as the man she adored penetrated her body, her heart, and her mind. Although her wrists were bound to a low branch and her legs were tossed over his shoulders, he did not 'fuck' her.

Instead, with their eyes and lips locked, they made love – slow, sweet, and passionate...

Chapter 21

The sound of dry heaving and sobbing woke her. Closer to comatose than consciousness, Zoey passed it off as part of a dream. Until it struck her that she wasn't dreaming.

Gianna!

Sitting up, she held her breath and listened. *Please...let me be wrong.* She wasn't. Whipping back the covers, she raced from her bedroom to the bathroom in the hall. Gianna was where she'd found her too many times before: on her knees, white knuckling the toilet and retching yellow bile. When her best friend lifted her head from the porcelain bowl and looked at her, Zoey was even more horrified than usual. A burst of adrenaline amped up her already nervous nervous system. Something was very wrong.

"Oh my god! Geeg, what happened?"

While the mess of mascara and clammy, ghost-like pallor were ghastly, they at least came as no surprise. With the gift of chronic Bulimia, such aberrations were part of the package. The matted tangle of hair and torn blouse, however, were not. Nor was the walnut sized goose egg on her jaw.

What the fuck?

Without another word, she ran for a blanket and an ice pack. Wrapping the former around Gianna's shoulders and pressing the latter to her face, she helped her to her bedroom. She pulled back the covers, undressed her as gently as she could, and tucked her in. It wasn't until she pressed a warm cup of tea into her freezing cold hands that she uttered her first words. Her beautiful voice was a cracked whisper.

"He hit me, Zoey."

Zoey's stomach dropped. She said nothing, just held her friend close and waited. When it came, it came in a gush.

"His name is William. William Waters. If you haven't heard of him, you've probably seen his work. He's a photographer. His stuff's in all the magazines. Anyway, he made me promise not to tell anybody about him to protect his precious reputation. His *married* reputation. But after this? *Fuck him and fuck that!*"

Gi swiped at her eye, took a sip of tea, and continued.

"I told you the other night that he told me to stop 'nagging' him for sex. That it was unattractive for a woman to, as he put it – *pressure* a man. As you know, I was embarrassed and more than a little confused. It made no sense. Yes, I asked him why he didn't show more affection. I'm Italian, we're demonstrative. But, *sex?* I never once said a word about sex."

"Of course you didn't, baby."

When Gianna had knocked on her door at four thirty in the morning, Zoey had been tickled pink. At first. She figured her old friend was back to her exuberant self and wanted to share details of her latest escapade. That wasn't the case. She'd suggested then that Gi dump him, that it sounded like he had a 'jerk' streak a mile wide. She deserved so much better.

If only she'd listened.

"I just don't understand, cara. Most men are all over me. William never touches me, although he sure talks a good game. You know—how perfect I am for him, how he can't wait to get his hands on me, how he's going to blow my mind, blah, blah, blah..."

"Gi, you need to call the police."

White as her sheets already, Gianna blanched.

"But, what if it was an accident, cara? He swore up and down that it was."

Zoey was incredulous. And unconvinced.

"You see, he couldn't...he had trouble...well...he couldn't get it up. There's no polite way to say it. It was like he needed to prove something after the other night. He tried several times, failed several times, and eventually, turned his back to me. I didn't know what to do, so I leaned over to reassure him that it was okay. That's when he flipped back and his knuckles caught my jaw. He said it was because I'd moved and he hadn't realized it."

"Do you believe that? It sounds like bullshit to me, Gi."

Her hesitation spoke volumes.

"Well, whether I believe it or not, I can't ruin his life over a maybe. So, no polizia. What I *am* going to do is never see him again. When I got up to leave, he was even more agitated. He wanted me to say that I forgave him, and, to placate him, I did. But...he still wasn't satisfied."

Gianna turned to face her but avoided eye contact. She pressed the ice pack to her jaw with one hand and gnawed the already mangled cuticles on the other. There was something else, Zoey could tell. Something she wasn't sure she wanted to share. *What could be worse than a punch to the face?* Alarmed, Zoey forced her features into a comforting smile. She didn't rush her, wasn't at all sure she wanted to know.

"Dio mio, Zoey, as I was leaving he called me a puta, a...a...whore. 'A worthless whore, just like the rest of them', as he put it. Have you ever in your life heard anything so hideous?"

* * * * *

As a matter of fact, she had. Word for word. It wasn't something a girl forgot.

When Gianna finally dozed off, Zoey tip-toed back to her own bed. Wired on adrenalin and shock, sleep eluded her.

You're a worthless whore...

Even before the words were out of Gi's mouth, her mind had back-flipped ten years. How could it not? In the one text she'd read, Billy Pickton had used the exact same words in the exact same order. What were the odds? Tossing and turning, she tried to convince herself they were pretty good. After all, women were called such things, and worse, every day. Disgusting but true. It was what came next that bothered her most.

Just like the rest of them...

Was she being ridiculous? This wasn't ten years ago, it was now. They weren't talking about Billy Pickton, prom king and football hero who'd left for law school with a pocket full of scholarships. They were talking about William Waters, photographer extraordinaire. The odds were excellent that he was just one more misogynistic dickhead in a world full of them.

Supporting herself on one elbow, she punched the tar and feathers out of her pillow, still hoping to catch a merciful couple hours of sleep. Somewhat lulled, her breathing began to slow and her muscles to relax. She willed herself to think happy thoughts, specifically those that revolved around Ash Harrington and her tenderized rump.

Yet, try as she might, her mind had a will of it's own. It was busy scribbling notes about Billy Pickton. Where *had* he settle after college? Was he married? What was the name of his practice? She assumed that by now, he was the slick-tongued senior partner of some huge – and hugely slimy—law firm. Pickton, Pervert and Dirtbag sounded about right.

A grainy image of Billy standing in her parent's doorway with a camera around his neck flashed before her eyes. On the threshold of oblivion, sleep overtook her before the image could attain gray matter...

Chapter 22

He sat motionless on the park bench, Indulgent Smile arranged on his face. The neighbors might notice the attentive parent watching his little princess play in the sandbox. They'd never suspect that beneath the candy-coated exterior, he was seething with a fury so intense, his eyes bulged from their sockets. Systematically, he cracked his oversized knuckles. With each savage snap, he envisioned Gianna's neck.

Who the fuck did that whore think she was?

In the sandbox, his daughter was madly shovelling her way to the earth's core. With any luck she'd succeed, fall in, and never be seen again. For a moment, his mind toyed with that improbable but still delightful scenario, one of dozens he'd envisioned over the five years of her life. He deserved a goddamned medal for not stuffing a pillow into her face the day she came home from the hospital. It would have been so simple to hold it there until her little legs stopped kicking. He'd fought the compulsion every day since.

On the other hand, it was nice to have something to look forward to...

Giving his head a shake, he nudged the recurrent fantasy onto the back burner and reduced the heat to simmer. He still needed the kid.

As with his parents, he felt no kinship to either Ana or her mother. That one was his child and the other his spouse didn't mean shit. He would use them, and when they were no longer useful, he would lose them. It was that simple. His DNA was MIA when the chromosome that connected one human being to another was handed out. When emotion was absent from the equation, the solution became wonderfully uncomplicated. Self-preservation was the name of the game. Everything and everyone else were expendable pawns – the means to a glorious end.

The shrewdest predators understood the importance of maintaining a low and respectable profile. His had been ten years in the making. He'd sacrificed much to ensure that he was looked past – or through—to whichever ne'er-do-wells lived down the road.

Wife – *Check.*

Kid – *Check.*

Church on Sundays – *Check, check.*

See? Just your everyday average Joe, folks – every conceivable shade of boring. Ignoring the angry throb at his temples, he polished up his Indulgent Smile and waved back at Ana.

"You there yet?"

"Almost I think, daddy."

Checking his phone, there were no messages from Gianna – an ominous sign. On any other day, half a dozen would be awaiting his leisure. No question, last night was a fiasco, but he'd done a masterful job of explaining away the intentional uppercut to her jaw. Nobody could blame him for being pissed. That's what she got for goading a man, trying to ridicule him into fucking her. There wasn't a man alive that could work it up for that scrawny skank.

Rubbing his knuckles, an impromptu sneer forced the arranged smile from his face. The slut had gotten off easy. If he weren't so disciplined, her emaciated carcass would be rotting in a garbage bin by now.

Nonetheless, it would appear that further damage control was in order. He wasn't going to kill himself over it, but he'd throw a few texts her way and see what developed. After all, he didn't *need* her to attain his ultimate objective, but there was no question she sweetened the pot. He could just imagine the look on Zoey's face after learning that her best friend had been tortured and sodomized – all in *her* honor. He wanted her to hear every detail of how, eventually, he choked the life from her battered body. *Slowwwly.* He relished sharing the experience with her.

Perhaps he would do so as she was spreading her ass cheeks in preparation for her own 'experience'...

And, just like that, after refusing to show a single sign of life the night before—his limp dick turned to titanium. Uncrossing his legs, he adjusted his pants to accommodate the abrupt expansion. At the same time, he unholstered his phone to text Gianna. Without so much as a how-do-you-do, his fickle cock deflated faster than a popped balloon. A whispered reprimand was in order.

"Gee. Thanks for the support, buddy. You think I'm having fun?"

Me: *Hey, baby. I'm missing you. I thought we kissed and made up?(happy face)*

No response.

Me: *I didn't sleep all night, thinking of you. Of us... (happy face, happy face)*

Nothing.

Me: *I feel bad enough, babe, please don't shut me out...I couldn't bear it...(sad face)*

FUCK!

And, then, just as he was about to give up...

Gianna: *I never want to see you again!*

The master manipulator within grinned. He was so fucking good!

Me: *Pookums. You can't mean that. You must know I'd never intentionally do anything to hurt you (sad face, sad face)*

Gianna: *My aching jaw aside, do you even remember what you said to me? (sad face)*

Oh, he did indeed.

Me: *You're adorable, babe. So naive. I'm truly sorry if my words upset you. It won't happen again. Promise.(happy face)*

No response.

Me: *You must know I'm falling in love with you...(heart)*

Gianna: *?? I do not...*

Me: *Let me pick you up for a coffee and I'll prove it... (heart, heart)*

Nothing.

Me: *Last night I told my wife I want a divorce...*

Chapter 23

Tonight, she meant to knock his socks off. Sporty Spice was sitting this one out. She was going full-on Posh – with a little Scary thrown in for extra oomph.

Up to her earlobes in bubbles, Zoey giggled at the reference to the girl group. When she was little, she worshipped the ground they walked on – even using a few bars of *Wannabe* in an early floor exercise routine. Dad used to dance to their videos with her, not that the jerking, twerking thing he did could be categorized as dancing. Sometimes she'd laugh so hard she'd collapse in a heap, tears running down her face. He always said she got her rhythm from her mother.

God, she missed him.

Before her thoughts turned maudlin, she lifted her freshly manicured tootsies past the waterline and wriggled them until the bubbles slid away. For the first time in her life, she had a hankering to look more feminine, and a pedicure was a great place to start. Gianna had done a magnificent job, painting on two layers of Lady of the Night Crimson and finishing it off with a clear top coat. Assessing the effect from the opposite end of the tub, she deemed it damned sexy. She could imagine the impact in four-inch high, open-toe sling-backs—the precarious footwear Gianna insisted she wear for the occasion. While she could never squeeze into one of her roommate's size zero dresses, her shoes were another story. It was like their feet came from the same mold: size seven and a half, B width, high instep, slight supination.

What they did not share was the ability to ambulate in

killer, sky-high stilettos. Where Gianna strutted, she teetered. They'd both be holding their breath that she made it though the evening without breaking her neck.

Pulling the plug, she rinsed off under the shower and stepped out of the tub to towel off.

When Gi heard that she and Ash were going out on the town for the first time as a couple, her face became more animated than it'd been all day. Other than the purple bruise along her jawline and her red-rimmed eyes, her smile was a beautiful thing to behold. There'd been so few of them lately. Instead of smiling back, though, Zoey gnawed her bottom lip, frowning.

"Zoey. Baby. Stop worrying. I'll be fine, I already am. I'm just going to do my nails, maybe call Peggy to chat for a bit. I'm done with jerk-off married men, that much I can promise. "

Gianna knew her so well, she'd read her mind. Despite her assurances, she tried again.

"But, I don't have to go, it's really no big deal. Ash and I can go another time. If you feel like you need company, hun, I'm your girl. We could order in and watch a movie."

"Are you kidding me, cara? There's only one reason anyone cancels a reservation at Vessuvio's. They've died! It's the best Italian on the planet, better than in Italy – pardon the profanity. Your man must have pulled some pretty major strings to get in on such short notice. Not only are you going, cherie, I've already appointed myself your official stylist. Lord knows you need one."

Was this the same person from whom she couldn't coax a good morning earlier? Relieved that her friend was in such high spirits, Zoey still looked forward to her parents arriving in a couple days. After she called, they booked the earliest fight available flight from Sicily, which included a layover in New York.

She'd giggled as Gianna gave her an exaggerated once over. The pained expression on her face when she finished was priceless.

"Are you planning on wearing sweat pants and sneakers, cara mia? Or, maybe you plan on kicking it up a notch? A skort and sandals, perhaps?"

"Come on, Gi. It can't be that bad."

"Don't 'come on' me, girl! You're right, it's not that bad. It's worse!"

It was all Zoey could do to keep a straight face.

"Don't come on me?"

It took Gianna a second to realize what she'd said, but, when she did, they both cracked up. So went the remainder of the afternoon.

Finally, with dramatic make-up applied and irrepressible curls restrained – at least for the time being –Zoey blinked into the full-length mirror. She hardly recognized herself. Ash Harrington made her feel like a beautiful, desirable woman, and tonight, she looked the part, as well. While the dress was conservative compared to the shoes, the combination was classic, clean—and hot as hell. The long sleeved jersey knit stopped a few inches above her knees. Normally loose and flowy, tonight it clung to her every curve courtesy of the thick belt Gianna added at the last second.

"Mon dio, cara! Time to stop hiding those big, beautiful boobies, si? I swear, I'm going to burn every one of those hideous sports bras. And the skorts. Ash will thank me. Which reminds me, when am I going to meet this god of a man that managed to melt the ice queen?"

As if on cue, the security buzzer went off.

"How 'bout right now?"

Gianna looked stricken. One might think she'd been offered a french fry.

"Now? Pazzo! Have you looked at me lately?"

Chuckling, Zoey hugged her best friend, careful to avoid the painful looking bruise. Grabbing a jewel-encrusted clutch and a pashmina wrap – both courtesy of Gianna—she tottered to the door.

"Do you want me to wake you when I get home? It could be late."

"But, of course, cherie. I'll be waiting!"

And with that, Zoey double bolted the door from the outside. If it weren't for the damned heels, she'd have skipped to the front foyer to meet Ash...

Chapter 24

The candlelit booth was secluded, as was every table in Vessuvio's Ristorante. With hand painted backdrops of Venetian canals and Tuscan vineyards, l'amore was the main course. Chef Antonio's exquisite culinary creations served as appetizers, and—who knew what was possible for dessert.

Marinating in her own juices, Zoey couldn't wait to find out.

Tuxedoed waiters hovered as unobtrusively as shadows, appearing a split second before a patron realized they needed or wanted for something. Of course, the sound system was superb. Heart-rending ballads resonated as though they were piped in straight from a quaint cafe on the Amalfi Coast. Closing her eyes, she imagined the tang of salt water and love in the air.

"One day, my love, I'll take you to Italy for dinner."

He'd met her in the foyer. When she'd lurched from the elevator, his thick forearm was there to support her. Good thing, too. One look at Ash and she'd gone weak in the knees. A knot of desire unfurled in her belly, molten lava hot. Her panties didn't stand a snowball's chance in hell of withstanding the heat.

At six foot four and closer to three hundred pounds than two, Ash looked like he'd just stepped from the pages of Esquire. The linen suit fit his impossibly broad shoulders to a T. Slate grey, it was a shade darker than his textured shirt, which in turn was a shade darker than his Windsor-knotted tie. A black leather belt and loafers completed the ensemble, breaking with the monochromatic theme. To contrast, a gold band encircled the ring finger of his right hand, wide enough to reach from knuckle to knuckle. The six Olympic rings were engraved on the face, punctuated by two diamonds – one for each gold medal he'd won, she assumed. He wore just enough cologne to entice.

And, oh, my, she was nothing if not enticed. If it weren't for his arm, she'd be swooning. If it weren't for Gianna's shoes, she'd be humping his perfectly pleated leg. She coughed, nearly choking on the thought, not to mention the image it evoked. Most shocking was how both appealed to the brazen hussy within. Ash's voice was a welcome distraction from that telling truth.

"To new beginnings, babygirl. And might I add, you look..."

His eyes were all over her. Her hair, pedicured toes – protuberant breasts – nothing escaped him. Her nipples hardened under his scrutiny.

"You look just fucking amazing!"

She hadn't noticed the stem of white daffodils until he hoisted it like a toast. Holding it to her nose, she lowered her eyes to hide the sudden swell of tears. Her heart melted in her chest even as she feared the same destiny for her mascara. This man was dangerously fall-in-loveable.

"Mmm...thank you, handsome. To new beginnings!"

He'd helped her out to his SUV then, laughing at her inelegant gait. Instead of waiting for her to clamber up into the passenger seat, he lifted her by the waist and deposited her there. Giggling, her instincts took over. She cupped his face with both hands and kissed him. He kissed her back with a soul searing mix of ferocity and tenderness. They were both panting when their lips parted. While hers hung slack, his curled into a lecherous smirk.

"Be very careful, my love. The beast sleeps fitfully. Perhaps it's best you wait until after we've eaten to awaken him."

Three hours later, all that was left of the appetizers, salads, and a shared entree of spaghetti smothered in bay scallops and Chef Antonio's secret marinara sauce were two distended bellies and memories. Drunk on love, laughter, and plenty of wine, they sipped espressos and cuddled in what they now considered 'their booth'. She struggled to not blurt out that she loved him. Nestled at his side, she felt his eyes on her. Looking up, she met his gaze and sighed. It was perfect.

And, then, it wasn't...

"What happened, babygirl? It tears my heart out to see the pain in your eyes."

The panic began as a tremor in her stomach. Tearing her eyes from his, she was sitting bolt upright before better she knew it. *Real nonchalant, idiot!* Keeping with that theme, she jerked away when he reached for her. Dislodging a loose curl from her up-do, she knotted and unknotted it frantically.

"Whatever do you mean?"

"Your overreaction says you know exactly what I mean, darling. You hide it well– from the rest of the world. I'm not the rest of the world. I see confusion. Fear. Torment. You've never ventured far from the gym, never really dated. It doesn't take a PhD in psychology to figure out that something happened. Something traumatic."

Her breath caught when he paused to stroke her cheek, the only part of her face available to him other than her earlobe.

"I was terrified to share my secret with you, but I'm so

thankful I did. It, *you*, transformed my life. Now, it's your turn to trust me. I'd never hurt you, babe, I hope you know that."

The tremor of panic was gone, in its place a full-blown quake. Her temples were pounding like a set of snare drums, making it hard to breathe. Harder to think. His spot-on insight boggled the mind. She was in love with Ash, truly, madly, deeply. But, it wasn't that simple. He was digging up something she'd kept buried for a decade.

"I do know that, Ash. But, really, there's nothing to tell. Other than not making the team and losing my dad, of course. Maybe that's what you see?"

She turned again to face him, but was careful to avoid eye contact. Trying on a guileless smile, she found the fit tight and unnatural. Her entire face felt contorted. If she were fooling anyone, it wasn't Ash. If he pressed, she wasn't sure she could maintain the sham.

But, he didn't press.

"Forget I mentioned it, Zoey. Forgive me for prying. It's not my business."

She didn't correct him. Couldn't. Even if the hurt in his voice shredded her heart. By the time he dropped her off at her apartment, it felt like a giant goiter was lodged in her throat. This time it was Ash that didn't meet her eyes.

"Good night, Zoey."

So much for dessert...

Chapter 25

The backhand knocked her clean off the chair. Irina went sprawling, nearly taking the kid out in the process. There was a slight tug in his pants upon impact, but, certainly, nothing to do with desire. His wife repulsed him. On the other hand, a little random brutality never failed to get a rise out of him.

Thankfully, she'd gotten knocked up easy. With that repugnant mission accomplished, he'd never gone near her again. Isolated and ignorant, who was she gonna call?

Of course, during extended 'dry-spells' he might rape her with a dildo expressly designed to cause pain and deny pleasure. That would get him hard enough to whack off, at least. If he was lucky he might ejaculate three out of five times – the three out of five times he envisioned her face purple and cold to the touch.

The thought caused a second tug, this one much more robust.

There was no time for distractions, however. He had much to accomplish. Ignoring the 'perfect family' he'd created to camouflage his true passion, he turned back to his dinner. The rack of lamp was superb, as were the roasted potatoes and Mediterranean salad. Irina was an excellent cook, not that she'd had any choice in the matter. If he had to put up with a fucking wife, she would learn to cook his favorite dishes.

Like his parents, she was terrified of him, too terrified to do a damn thing about it. Without so much as a whimper, she climbed back onto her chair and picked up her fork. She finished everything on her plate, careful to not incur his wrath a second time.

Still, she'd become awfully curious of late. It began right after he told her to start packing. Since then, she'd been sticking her nose where it didn't belong, asking questions she'd never asked before. Like tonight, for instance. What the fuck was she doing asking about his plans for the evening?

Her sudden interest in his activities was just one more reason she would die a slow and painful death. He'd have to wait until they were out of the country, of course. When his work here was done, his name would echo across the land, and not for some moronic photo spread in some moronic magazine, either. He was going to go down in history. The grimy masses would speak of him in hushed, quavering tones. He would read about it from his cozy hideaway in Croatia. If all went according to plan, maybe he'd remarry and start again.

A third tug indicated that his dick was on board with the idea.

Ahhh...life was good!

With a long, satisfied belch, he pushed his chair away from the table. Gianna hadn't texted him, the cunt. Still, all was not lost. She knew where he'd be and when. If she showed, he would have an enjoyable, if demanding night ahead of him. If she didn't, he would have a plan to reformulate.

"Bye daddy."

MOTHER FUCKING FUCK!

Ana had witnessed her mother's beatings all her life. To her, it was business as usual. She'd learned the hard way that if she started wailing, she could expect the same. And yet, the kid always seemed happy to see him and sad to see him go.

Odd. There were times he almost wished he could let her live. But, considering she'd be motherless and he sure the fuck didn't want her, it was a non sequitur. Rummaging around for Father Face, he bestowed it upon his progeny then turned on his heel and left the room.

In his bedroom, he stripped off his clothes, leaving them where they fell. Joggling his soggy balls, he gazed downwards with real affection in his heart and spoke for the first time since arriving home.

"Are you ready for a little fun, my debaucherous crony in crime? Now, let's hope the dumb twat complies, eh?"

Setting the clippers to 'One', he buzzed his already buzzed scalp and chest. Kicking it down a notch, he gave his pubic area the same treatment. It wouldn't do to have a hair pulled out by its DNA-infused roots. The cops might be bumbling and clueless, but that didn't mean he should leave them a calling card with his particulars engraved.

At least, not until it was time...

Meeting the Chief of Police at that lame-ass poker game was a bonus worth every penny he'd purposely lost. Like a star-struck girl, the malleable Chief O'Malley had hung on his every word. He couldn't help but chuckle at the image of serial killer and police Chief, yukking it up over a friendly game of cards.

Like he said, bumbling and clueless.

Speaking of bumbling and clueless, how could the Chief's good buddy, Ash Harrington, not spring to mind? At the thought of Zoey's love interest, his teeth clamped together so hard his ears rang. He'd never had to deal with competition before. To say he was displeased was an understatement of colossal proportion. The idea of that dumb slab of beef with his girl infuriated him to the point of blind, murderous rage.

To stay calm, he cracked his knuckles and thought of the snapshots he would send the inconsolable boyfriend. If they didn't fuck him up for the rest of his life, nothing would.

Placated, he slipped into what he called his multipurpose 'ninja' outfit. Black from head to toe, the mock turtle and fitted pants allowed him to go from stylish suitor to cunning killer seamlessly.

He exited through the garage. Even next to the new model Porsche Spyder, the 1995 Lincoln Continental stood its ground. As black as his soul, it gleamed, every square inch detailed and customized. The wheels were the piece de resistance. Far too flashy for practical purposes, the twenty-two inch spinner rims drew the eye as surely as a pubescent girl's sprouting breasts. As far as he was concerned, both were impossible to resist.

But, the Lincoln's real attraction was its trunk space. Unlike the Porsche, there was more than enough to house a dead body or two. He didn't even have to remove the spare tire. Heading to the storage shed, he itemized what he would need in his head.

After the last fiasco – plenty of film.

Chloroform.

Flex cuffs.

Lube.

Plastic tarp.

Duct tape.

Knife.

Just your regular, run of the mill party favors. As always, his trusty Glock was tucked away in the glove compartment.

With holster and registration present and accounted for, he was just another law-abiding, gun-toting citizen with the god-given right to protect himself from the criminal underbelly of society. He couldn't help but giggle.

By the time he'd checked off each item, his dick was a concrete pole weeping in his pants. Still smiling, he turned on his favorite rock station. Belting out Highway to Hell at the top of his lungs, he stepped on the gas.

Speaking of highways to hell, he had a goody bag to pack...

Chapter 26

"Gi?"

She tapped on the door with one hand, holding Gianna's shawl, purse, and tootsie-tormenting heels in the other. Rolling her ankles in sweet relief, she waited for her beleaguered roomie to respond. In truth, she had no desire to chat. If she hadn't promised, she'd be in bed by now, kicking her own ass around la-la-land.

The thought of Ash's 'interrogation' caused the same suffocating panic she'd experienced at Vessuvio's, only now it was tinged with annoyance. Had she the slightest inkling of what was on his mind, she might have been able to brace herself. Instead, it came blazing out of left field, a radioactive fireball aimed straight for the tender underbelly of her psyche. There was nothing to do but duck. To him, it must have looked like she was pulling away.

Maybe she was.

After all, even if it were possible to see the 'torment' in her eyes as he'd insisted, this wasn't a game of tit for tat. It was Ash's choice to share, it was her prerogative not to. For him to expect otherwise was unfair and presumptuous. Billy Pickton wasn't just some dirty little secret, he was the stuff of nightmares. Her nightmares.

"Gi, I'm home early. You sleeping, girl?"

She tapped again, a little harder this time. Still no response.

If she could sleep through this racket, she must really need the Z's. A wave of relief swept over her. Her best friend was clearly on the mend. No asshole was going to keep her down for long. She'd been her old bubbly self earlier, even putting on a little make up. Now, she was sleeping like a baby.

She wouldn't wake her.

Filling her lungs, she blew the air out in one long whoosh. They'd catch up in the morning. It was soon enough to rehash the particulars of what had turned out to be a disastrous evening. Right now all she wanted was to stick her head under a pillow and pray for oblivion to take her. A quick check on her bestie and she'd be halfway there. Cracking the door a smidge, she peeked in. It took a moment to realize that the bed was empty.

What the...?

Not firing on all cylinders, her brain was slow to process the unexpected data. Stepping into the room, she flicked on the lights and did a full three-sixty. Considering the modest dimensions, it was a preordained exercise in futility. At least by the time she'd come full circle, her mind had caught up with reality.

Gianna was gone.

But...where did she go? Returning the borrowed accessories to the closet, she recalled her words from that afternoon: *I'm just going to do my nails, maybe call Peggy to chat for a bit...*

That was it!

Releasing her pulverized lip, she smiled for the first time. She was right, Gi was back to her old self. A social butterfly of mythological proportion, she hated, hated, *hated* staying in. It wouldn't take much prodding to get her out. In fact, she was most likely the prodd-er, not the prod-ee. Plus, after what she'd been through, she'd feel safe with 'Mama' Peggy.

They'd probably gone to Turn Outs, a quiet, non-alcoholic club frequented by an odd mix of athletes and ex-ahcoholics. It was owned by Jock, Peggy's husband. Jock wasn't his real name, but she'd never heard anyone refer to him otherwise. Not even Peggy. In close proximity to the NGTC, Turn Outs was like a second home. They made oxygen smoothies to die for.

Maybe she'd slip into something more comfortable and join them. She hadn't seen Peggy in ages. Retrieving her phone, she tried Gi's cell first, then Peggy's. Both rang until their voice mails kicked in. She left messages on each. Checking the time, she considered and then rejected the idea of trying Peggy at home. There was no use heading over to Turn Outs, either. Which was fine. Beyond exhausted, her feet, her head, and her shoulder throbbed. Not to mention her heart. Despite her tough talk, she missed Ash already.

Dragging herself down the hallway, she washed the unaccustomed makeup from her face and brushed her teeth. Even though it hadn't rang, she checked her phone. With nothing from Gianna, Peggy, or Ash, it was time to file this day under 'Better Luck Tomorrow' and hit the hay.

In bed, an unsettling chill crept up her spine. Odd, that Gi wouldn't call or at least leave a note. She had to know she'd be worried, coming home to find her gone. On the other hand, thanks to unforeseen and unfortunate circumstances, Zoey was home way earlier than expected. Much earlier. Gi probably thought she'd be back with plenty of time to spare.

But, something else was niggling. If she was to get any rest, it needed to be addressed.

What if...?

NO!

It was an appalling thought, contemplated and rejected.

Gianna was a little insecure, but, not *that* insecure. If she'd gone out with William Waters tonight, Zoey would personally kick her butt around the block.

I'm done with jerk-off married men, that I can promise.

A promise is a promise. Right?

Right.

Dismissing the ominous feeling, Zoey closed her eyes and forced her mind to go blank...

✶ ✶ ✶ ✶ ✶

What time is it?

Zoey jolted upright from a deep dreamless sleep. Disoriented, she squinted at the clock, shocked to discover it was five thirty in the morning. She'd been sleeping for six blissful hours. But, what woke her? And, why was her heart beating out of her chest? No phones were ringing, no alarms were buzzing, no sirens were screeching. It was absolute silence melded with absolute darkness.

When she figured it out, she catapulted out of bed, driven by adrenaline. The ominous feeling was back and this time, with a vengeance. Her throat constricted for reasons unknown. She could hardly breathe. Sucking for air, she willed the muscles surrounding her windpipe to relax.

What the fuck?

With one catastrophe averted, her distended bladder threatened another. Clammy from exertion, she raced for the toilet. It didn't hit her until she was on the commode and out of imminent danger. Gianna's jacket was missing from it's peg. She hadn't come home. Wiping and flushing, she didn't bother with washing. She covered the few feet to her girlfriend's bedroom with trepidation in her heart. With a deep breath she pushed open the door, praying Gi was in bed where she belonged.

She wasn't.

Frozen to the spot, Zoey tried to contain her panic. Gianna was a big girl. This wouldn't be the first time she'd stayed out all night. She could take care of herself. The list of platitudes went on and on, each more meaningless than the last.

Screw containment.

Her girlfriend was in trouble – she could feel it...

Chapter 27

If she was panicked before, she was near hysterical now. From the corner of her eye she noticed her hands. The knuckles were bloodless. At ten and two, they clutched the steering wheel like a drowning woman clutches a buoy. They were trembling so badly when she left home, she probably shouldn't be driving.

Fuck that!

Already exceeding the speed limit, she pressed down on the gas pedal yet again. She needed a police station and she needed it now. There'd been no word from Gianna. She hadn't driven, her car was still in its usual spot out back. More alarming, her phone was now going straight to voicemail. What she'd learned between finding her best friend's bed empty and squealing out of the garage on this abhorrent endeavor had her mind cartwheeling and the hair on the back of her neck bristling.

She'd raced for her phone, needing to reach Peggy even if it was five thirty in the morning. It was ringing by the time she reached it.

"Zoey? It's me, Peggy. I got your message honey, but, I'm a little confused. I didn't hear from Gianna last night. Was I supposed to?"

She'd screamed into the phone then, her voice a decibel she didn't recognize.

"Peggy! Gianna's...Gianna's gone! I don't...I can't..."

"Zoey, baby, You need to slow down. You're not making any sense. What do you mean 'gone'? Start from the beginning honey. Tell mama Peggy what happened."

After a couple of deep breaths, she managed to tell her everything. Everything she knew, at least. She told her about Gi's abrupt change in personality after meeting a creepy married man. About her bulimia returning. About the knot on her jaw and how it came about. Finally, she told her about about their last conversation.

"She said she was going to call you. Oh, my god, I should never have left her alone!"

Peggy rattled off the same platitudes she'd rattled off to herself just a few moments before. Gianna's a big girl, it's not like she hasn't stayed out all night before, blah, blah, blah. But, Peggy hadn't known about Billy Pickton and William Waters. How could she?

At the time, neither had she.

At the time, she'd still had the luxury of optimism, and she'd wallowed in it. Of course, the misogynistic prick would bring her home at some point, just like he always did. Maybe this time, the only damage would be a blow to her dignity – not her face. She meant to have a word or two with Gi when she got home, tell her how worried she'd been.

But, all that was before she sat down at the computer to ask the Google gods a few nagging questions. It didn't take long for the all-knowing search engine to make a mockery of her optimism, leaving her numb, weak and nauseous. What she discovered seemed too incredible to be true, yet, the laundry list of coincidences screamed otherwise.

Suspicion dawned as she scoured the internet for anything she could find on William Waters, her chief suspect in Gianna's mysterious disappearance. His name popped up for the first time just nine years ago. Search as she might, she could find nothing previous. Going forward, however, there was a myriad of information chronicling his accomplishments as a photographer, husband and father. He was also an active member of his church. By all accounts, the man was a model citizen, respected in both his profession and his community.

But, Zoey knew better. She knew that at the very least, he was a cheater. And, despite Gianna's denials, she was convinced the crack to her jaw was the work of an abuser.

Zooming in on a grainy picture, she did a double-take, her already overwhelmed mind scrambling for traction. *Was it possible?* Still not believing her eyes, she leaned closer. There was no mistaking the tilt of that head, the singular glint in those eyes. Aloof and arrogant, it was as though he looked down on everyone and everything around him. At sixteen, she'd mistaken that exact same look for sophisticated and sexy.

Certainty hit her like a ton of bricks: *William Waters and Billy Pickton were the same person!*

Recoiling in horror, it struck her that Billy was a common diminutive for William. Dread gripped her heart with cold, malevolent fingers. Blood turned to ice in her veins. *What was happening?* If Gi had walked through the door at that moment, she'd have wrapped her in a bear hug so tight, she'd need to peel her off. Conquering the urge to run and hide, Zoey forced herself to compare the man to the boy she'd tried for ten unsuccessful years to forget.

She saw no outward resemblance, and felt the faintest ray of hope return. The Billy Pickton she'd known had flowing, shoulder-length hair. William Waters had a buzz cut. Billy had a snub nose, crooked from too many football injuries. William Waters' was narrow and straight. Billy's eyes were oval shaped, William Waters' were unnaturally round, as though toothpicks were holding up his eyelids.

Could she have been wrong? *Please god, let me be wrong!* After all, they really looked nothing alike.

Her fingers flew over the keyboard. She couldn't type Billy's name into the search bar fast enough. What she found annihilated all hope once and for all.

There were no photos and just one brief mention, but it was enough. Too much, in fact. Billy dropped out of college near the end of his first year. It was prefaced by some murky 'off-campus incident' involving a woman. Zoey could well imagine the nature of the 'incident', but found nothing further. Three weeks later, Billy hadn't just dropped out of school – he'd dropped off the face of the planet. He wasn't on social media. He wasn't listed in any phone book or directory. He wasn't anywhere.

That was nine years ago.

As the last puzzle piece fell into place, she was no longer able to hold it together. With all avenues of hope closed, her teeth began to chatter. Sweat poured from her body in rivulets, alternating hot and cold. The world slipped into slow-motion mode. She knew she was going into shock. Cupping her hands over her nose and mouth, she forced herself to take long deep breaths.

Billy Pickton slash William Waters had single-handedly ruined her life. She wasn't about to sit idly by and let him ruin Gianna's, as well...

* * * * *

"Here's your copy of the complaint, miss. We understand your concern, but your roommate is an adult. An adult with a history of not coming home, from what you've told us. If you haven't heard from her after twenty-four hours, we'll open a missing person investigation."

The pimply-faced rookie stuffed the document into her numb hand. His fake, by-the-book smile caused a couple of the riper pustules to ooze. Struck dumb by his polite indifference, all she could do was stare. At least the bullshit smile disappeared under the scrutiny.

"Have a nice day, miss."

The import of his words combined with his demeanor was too much. She was done with this bozo. She turned to the senior officer to his right. Surely, he could put two and two together and come up with four?

"Please, Officer Ketchins. Twenty-four hours could be too late. I swear to you, if I hadn't woken up when I did, this guy would have *raped* me! What *if* Gianna is with him? Are you willing to take that chance?"

"Miss Benton. It's like Officer Krevetzky said, we understand your concern. But, you have to understand our position, as well. At this juncture, our hands are tied. Legally tied. You come in here with a tale straight out of Twilight Zone and you expect us to roll out in full force? To do what, exactly? Raid a citizen's home? Business? Both?"

Officer Ketchins cut her off before she could respond. He was right on the money, though – that's exactly what she expected. In fact, why weren't they half-way there already?

"This Mr. Waters or Mr. Pickton or whatever you want to call him – is a private citizen with rights. If he chooses to have plastic surgery, that's his right. If he chooses to change his name, that's also his right. Until he breaks an actual law, he has the same rights as you and I. You didn't make a formal complaint against him ten years ago, therefore we only have your word that anything untoward happened. I'm not saying that it didn't. I'm saying that even if it did, the statute of limitations was up years ago.

Do you see where I'm going with this, miss? He's broken no laws. Neither has your roommate, who has every right to go out with whomever she likes. She has no obligation to notify you or anyone else."

When she still didn't budge, Officer Ketchins sighed, hefted himself out of his seat and lumbered to the door. Holding it open, he peered at her meaningfully, his lips compressed into a thin white line. If compressed lips could speak, Officer Ketchins' would be telling her to get the fuck out. *Now.*

Her head spun. She'd done everything but back flips to get them to understand. If it would help, she'd do the back flips too, shoulder be damned. Rising, she steadied herself against the desk and left. Her throat was so dry, she couldn't swallow the sour bile that was shooting into it like a geyser.

"Try to relax, miss. Ninety-nine percent of the time, it turns out to be nothing. Your friend is probably at home right now, wondering where you are."

Officer Ketchin's voice of experience trailed her out of the building. *Ninety-nine percent of the time?* Those odds didn't impress her much. Ten years ago, she was given a ninety-nine percent chance of making the Olympic team.

She had a terrible feeling the odds weren't good enough for Gianna, either...

Chapter 28

"At sixteen years old, I was drugged and assaulted. At least, I believe I was assaulted. I've never told anybody, ever. Until today."

Drugged? Assaulted? Jesus fucking Christ!

He hadn't been expecting anyone, certainly not Zoey. Still in pajama bottoms, he'd been sprawled on the couch rehashing their disastrous night at Vessuvio's and nursing a third cup of coffee. Black and bitter, it was the perfect reflection of his mood. The fifty-two inch television was tuned to a local news station, the volume muted. Unseeing, his eyes followed the banners crawling across the bottom of the screen while his mind indulged in a game of 'What If". It was all the rage with the self-debasing crowd.

What if I wasn't such an egotistical dickhead?

What if I could mind my own fucking business?

What if I kept my big mouth shut?

Of course, as with any game worth playing, the best was saved for last...

What if I'm head over heels, ass over teakettle, cow jumps over the moon in love with Zoey Benton?

Fuck, he regretted the can of worms he'd opened at Vessuvio's. The stricken look on Zoey's face said it all: *You've gone too far, buddy boy. Back away before someone gets hurt.* If only he'd listened. But, no. In his infinite lack of wisdom, he'd forged ahead, prodding and pushing for more. The walls she erected were immediate and insurmountable, the chill between them so glacial he'd swear he saw his breath. The original plan was to bury his head between her legs and have her for dessert. And breakfast, if she were available. Instead, he'd buried his head up his own ass, making certain it was well and properly lodged.

Fuuuck!

Today, he'd cleared his calendar and wasn't expecting anyone. When the buzzer rang, he almost spilled his coffee. To see Zoey in the foyer was music to his eyes. But...something was wrong. She was pacing circles around the square entranceway, hunched over and hugging herself. Even with the grainy video, he could make out the shimmer of tears on her cheeks. Terror radiated from her in waves.

"Wait there, babygirl. I'm coming down to get you."

Now, ensconced between his legs with her back pressed to his bare chest and his arms wrapped around her, she continued to shake like a leaf. Her face was cadaver white, her hands ice cube cold despite the mug of hot coffee he'd installed between them. She felt so fragile against him, he was afraid she might break apart. It wasn't possible, but he held her closer still.

"Zoey, baby, I'm so, *so* sorry. I can't imagine how awful it must have been for you. And, keeping it locked inside for all these years? I'm here now, my love. Nothing you can say will change that *or* how I feel about you. You're stuck with me, through thick and thin, sickness and health, as long as you'll have me. But, tell me, darling, what happened between last night and this morning?"

Her voice was so soft he had to strain to hear it.

"Gianna is missing. The police don't seem to care. I believe she's with the same man."

WHAT?

Even after a decade, the odds of that happening naturally

were beyond astronomical.

"The same man? Are you positive? Babygirl, I need you to start at the beginning and tell me everything. Take your time and leave nothing out. I may know just the person who can help."

The story she told broke his heart.

"His name was Billy Pickton and I was crazy about him. When he asked me to senior prom, I felt like the luckiest girl in the world. He was one of, if not *the* most popular boy in school and I was just a flat-chested freshman who attended half-time."

She paused to take a breath, her unblinking eyes glued to the muted TV. It was as though she was spiralling back in time, reliving every emotion. With her back to him, she didn't have the added burden of eye contact. Burying his face in her hair, he kissed the top of her head. Although he didn't rush her, he wasn't nearly as calm as he pretended. *What the fuck was going on here?* His gut told him that whatever it was, it wasn't good.

"At the time, I was training for World's. Between living in the dorm five days a week and training seven hours a day, we didn't see much of each other. I didn't know him very well and I didn't care. I was young, naive, and so bedazzled by the Emperor's new clothes that I didn't see the naked truth beneath. Dad came with me to shop for a dress. He was so cute, trailing along behind me from one store to the next."

There was a hitch in her melancholy voice.

"I wish he could have met you, Ash, seen how happy you make me."

And, with that, she twisted her body just enough to plant a soft kiss on his cheek. His throat closed. Tears threatened.

The Goddess Venus must have passed a note to her good buddy Cupid who, in turn, took direct aim at his heart.

"I love you Zoey Benton. Now, carry on, please."

His timing sucked, but he wasn't sorry he said it. After a moment of stunned silence, she snuggled into him and continued.

"When we arrived at the venue, it was madness. Stanchions and overwhelmed volunteers blocked long deserted hallways. It was nothing to slip past them and find an empty room far from the crowded auditorium. I didn't stop for a second to wonder where we were going or why. I just followed him like a lovestruck puppy."

"Somehow, he'd managed to smuggle in a small bottle of champagne. He pulled it out of his pants, popped the cork, and proceeded to wander around the room, looking for something. When he returned, he'd poured some into a plastic container which he handed to me."

Zoey's body tensed against his, her every muscle coiled. She swallowed twice before speaking again.

"The next thing I remember is waking up puking my guts out. My dress was disheveled and my...my panties were too. When I got home, I noticed a chunk of hair was missing, as if it'd been chopped off. To this day, I have no idea what actually happened. To use your word, it's tormented me ever since. What I do know is who's responsible and how a single evening with him impacted my life. And now, Gi's missing and the police don't care!"

He was so distraught at what she'd gone through, he wasn't connecting the dots.

"And, you think Gianna is with this Billy Pickton?"

This time, she spun around so violently, she broke free of

his arms.

"I do.   Except he's not Billy Pickton anymore.   He changed his name and gotten a ton of plastic surgery.   Now he's some big shot photographer named William Waters..."

Chapter 29

...Breaking News...Second Murder Victim Identified...
...Breaking News...Second Murder Victim Identified...

William Waters? Billy Pickton? Before Ash could even begin to process the surreal information, Zoey was screaming.

"Oh my god, oh my god! Turn it *up!*"

Investigative journalist Gabriel Montero was interviewing Percy O'Malley, Ash's good friend and Chief of Police. Whereas Ms. Montero was sleek, groomed, and professional, the same could not be said for the Chief. He took his style cues straight from Columbo, including the squint and the shuffling gait.

As much as their fashion acumen clashed, their facial expressions were a matched set. Their identical grimaces were an ominous foreshadowing of what was to come. 'The Nose' hid his apprehension just a hair better than the reporter. Her voice actually shook.

"We understand you have new information about the latest victim, Chief. What can you tell us?"

"The victim discovered two nights ago has been identified as thirty-five year old Roberta Perrin, nee Kettner. Her next of kin have been notified and an autopsy has been performed. The cause of death is ligature strangulation."

"Do we know if it's related to the Jersey Stefanson case?"

"Unfortunately, the similarities are inescapable. Ligature strangulation is rare, to say the least. To have two – possibly three – cases in a relatively short period of time is not a coincidence. And, while Ms. Perry wasn't directly associated with the sport of gymnastics, we feel it's important to note that her mother, Evelyn Thies, was one of the first American women to make a final event in an Olympic Games. We'll be holding a press conference in one hour to warn the public of a possible serial killer and what they can do to protect themselves until he's caught."

Zoey looked like she'd been hit by a train.

"Serial killer...? Please...god...nooo..."

"Is there anything else you can share with our audience at this time, Chief?"

Afraid of what might be coming, Ash pulled Zoey onto his lap and held her tight. He watched as the Chief hucked a luger into his throat then spit it into the gravel at his feet. He looked about as happy as a man having a heart attack.

"Yes. One other thing. An excavator operator at the east end landfill unearthed another body early this morning. Quite decomposed, no ID. We know that it's female. She was naked and her hair was chopped off like the others. We're searching the national archives for anything that fits the MO. Dark hair. Petite. At least two are connected to elite gymnastics."

Zoey's gasp was more of a sob. Her words echoed in his head: *When I got home, I noticed a chunk of hair was missing, like it'd been chopped off.* Zoey's eyes were the size of dinner plates. She was leaned forward, intent on every word.

"This is the first official confirmation we've received of their hair being cut off, Chief. Do you think..."

The famous O'Malley grunt of impatience cut her cold.

"That's all you're getting for now, Gabriel. I'll have more at the press conference, including the tip line number. See you then."

Horror was etched into Zoey's face. Her every word

dripped with it.

"I'm petite, have dark hair, and am connected to gymnastics. So is Gianna. Oh, my god! Billy Pickton is the serial killer!"

Her wail pierced his heart. More frightened than he'd ever been in his life, he felt helpless to comfort her.

"GIANNAAAA..."

＊ ＊ ＊ ＊ ＊

Ash got his shit together, and quick. Although his legs were slow to respond and his heart felt heavier than an anvil, he didn't have the luxury of inaction. There were things to do and people to see and every single second counted. Lives depended on it.

Speeding to the gym, he dialed Percy O'Malley's private number. *Hey Perc, remember that guy we played cards with the other night...?* After five unsuccessful attempts to reach him, he left a succinct voicemail: *Call me ASAP. I have information you need to hear.* No doubt, the Chief was in the middle of his press conference and, no doubt, Zoey was glued to his every word. He'd left her at his place with strict instructions to not move a muscle until he got back.

She was safe there, at least for the time being. He had to consider that Waters replacing Cassandra Taves at the photo shoot was something other than coincidence.

That Billy Pickton, the man he'd been introduced to as Will Waters, was a twisted serial killer boggled the mind. That the son of a bitch assaulted the woman he loved when she was just sixteen made his heart ache and his blood boil. *Just let me have him to myself for ten seconds – mano o coward.*

Sure, he'd struck him as odd at the photo shoot. Slimy even. But, a serial killer? *Fuck me!* It was beyond comprehension.

And yet, it was true. He was convinced beyond a shadow of a doubt. Zoey had laid out the sickening proof point by irrefutable point, her pupils dilated with shock.

While Pickton went off to college to become a lawyer, he'd also had a passion for photography.

He hurled the same insult at Gianna as he had at Zoey a decade before. Word for disgusting word.

And finally, the internet searches. There was no refuting the fact that where Pickton ended, Waters began. He'd even seen glimpses of that nasty 'look in his eyes' that had stopped Zoey in her tracks and propelled her to dig deeper.

Ash thanked the heavens above that she had, however harrowing the truth she'd unearthed. If her reporting Gianna missing was of no interest to a couple of short-sighted cops, the possibility that she was in the hands of the city's first ever serial killer was sure to have the entire department scrambling to find her.

Next, he called Mercedes. He needed his ex-wife to take Cherish far, far away from where a psychopath was stalking gymnasts and anyone connected to them. She picked up on the first ring.

"What trouble did that slut you're fucking get us into, Ash?"

He wondered what he ever saw in the mean-spirited woman.

"As usual, Mercedes, you don't have a clue what you're talking about and I don't have the time nor the inclination to correct you. Try to put your resentment aside for a moment and listen to what I'm saying. Our daughter is in danger by virtue of giving birth to her, so are you. Tune into WMTV if you haven't heard. I'm on my way to the gym to arrange around the clock security. Meet me there in an hour, max, bags packed. I'm flying the two of you to your mother's until this is over. Cherish can train with the *Gym-Max-Tics* team while she's there, I'll make the arrangements. You have one hour, Mercedes. Are we clear?"

Crystal clear, judging from her high pitched shriek.

Squealing into the gym's parking lot, he threw the SUV into park and was bounding for the doors before the engine stopped running. He still needed to call the airport and a private security company. He also needed to find a safe place for himself and Zoey.

Zoey...

Even as his legs pumped and his mind churned, she was at the forefront of his thoughts. He hadn't mentioned anything before he left, but he had a terrible sinking feeling. If everything was as it seemed, this Billy Pickton was a patient and meticulous planner. Not to mention a fucked in the skull psychopath. Adding up the facts, Ash flinched at the logical conclusion.

It all circled back to Zoey, he felt it in his bones. There was no hard proof, but, he was convinced that for the past ten years, the sick son of a bitch's primary objective was to finish what he'd started. With Zoey. Everything else was some kind of twisted dress rehearsal.

Or...foreplay...

Chapter 30

PING!
PING, PING!
PING!
PING!

Curled into a corner of Ash's couch, Zoey almost jumped out of her skin. There was only one person she knew that texted in fits and starts. Frantic, she dug her cell out from under the mountain of blankets and stared gobsmacked at the screen. Still not believing her eyes, she squeezed them shut, counted to three, then re-opened them one at a time.

Gi: *Cherie, where are you? (sad face)*

Gianna's words leaped out at her, accent and all. Blood pounded in her ears to where it overrode the din of the television. *Where am I?* Was she fucking serious?

Gi: *Missing you Zee (heart)*

Gi: *Tried to reach you but my phone died (sad face)*

Gi: *Time for a nap. See you soon, cara (wink face, wink face)*

Zoey's trembling fingers flew.

Me: *GI? OMG! GI! I've been out of my mind with worry!*

Gianna's response was immediate and just like her free-spirited friend.

Gi: *Don't be silly, bella. (lol)*

Gi: *You know me. I get cabin fever (wink face)*

Gi: *See you on the other side, babe*

Gi: *Nighty-night (heart, heart)*

Me: *Wait! Where were you? You didn't take your car...*

Me: *Gi?*

Kicking off the covers, Zoey leaped from the couch. She'd soared from the depths of despair to the pinnacle of euphoria in less than six seconds. Mind awhirl, sweet relief washed over her in waves, her clammy, goose-bumped skin attested to it. Grabbing her purse, she dashed out the door, down the stairs and into her car, feet barely touching the ground. Now that she knew Gianna was safe and none the worse for wear, she was going to *kill* her when she got home. There'd be no polite knocking this time, either. The girl had scared ten years off her life.

Pressing 'Hands Free', she dictated Ash's phone number into the device. That amazing man had taken complete control of an ugly situation, doing his utmost to put her mind at rest. She wasn't to worry. He'd take care of everything. The Chief of Police was a good friend of his. He had a direct line. Passing her the television remote and refilling her coffee, he made sure she had everything she needed before he left.

Mentally, she thank Mercedes for being senseless enough to let him go.

I shouldn't be more than an hour, hour and a half tops, babygirl. By the time I get back, the troops will be rallied with a name – or two – to work with. That scumbag will have nowhere to hide. He'd kissed the tip of her nose before straightening to leave. While his tone was confident, his furrowed brow and tight lips spoke to the charade. She'd grabbed for his wrist then, her two hands barely managing to wrap around its girth. He towered over her. Tilting her head back, she met his eyes. God, they were beautiful.

"I love you, too."

His expression took her breath away. For a moment, it pulled her free from the vortex of insanity she'd been sucked into. And, then, he was gone.

Hi, you've reached Ash. Leave a message and I'll get back to you...

Knowing he had his hands full, she did as instructed.

"Hi handsome. Great news. Gianna just texted. She's home, tired but safe. Btw, have I mentioned lately how much I adore you?"

Too impatient to drive around the block to park in her assigned stall, she pulled in front of her building and clicked on the four-ways. She wouldn't be long. She could probably give Gianna hell and a hug and still beat Ash back to his place. Tucking her purse under the seat, she hopped out of the car, locked it, and sprinted the few feet to the door. Based on heart rate alone, one would guess she'd just run a marathon at full tilt. It sure felt like she had. Bypassing the elevator, she took the stairs two and three at a time. The hinges on their apartment door screeched like nails on a chalkboard when she threw it open.

"Gi? Oh my god, girl, you'd best run!"

Laughing like a loon, she headed straight for Gianna's bedroom. Her peripheral vision, however, noted that the one coat hook remained empty. *What the...?* While the flutter in the pit of her belly was barely noticeable, the laughter died in her suddenly dry throat. Stopped dead in her tracks, Zoey took a good look around the apartment.

It was then that the hair on the back of her neck stood up. Crouching into a defensive stance with her feet staggered and her hands raised, she edged towards Gi's bedroom door...

Had she closed it in her mad dash to get to the police station?

She couldn't even think, never mind recall such a minute

detail. It wasn't minute anymore, however. Holding her breath, she twisted the knob until the latch clicked. Pushing it open with her toe, she hoped for the best but prepared for the worst. A surreal feeling of deja vu engulfed her. The flutter in her stomach was gone.

In its place was a Category Five hurricane...

Chapter 31

She had just enough time to register that the room was empty when the doorbell rang. Frozen to the spot, cold terror gripped her as the truth sunk in. *She'd been conned!* The implications were staggering, too staggering to fathom. Her brain and nervous system spun into overload. Until they had the opportunity to sort themselves out, Zoey was paralyzed.

One thing was certain. It wasn't Gianna at the door. She might be slow, she wasn't stupid. As much as it lacerated her heart, as much as she'd give anything to change it – one plus one always added up to two.

Based on that principle, Gianna was dead and Billy Pickton had killed her. And, now, he was after her.

At last, she crept to the kitchen. Her head came close to exploding with the effort it took to regulate her breathing. Pulling the longest knife she could find from the butcher block, she took up a position beside the front door. She may go out of her way to not hurt a fly, but if Billy Pickton was at the door, it'd be her pleasure to run him through. With her back pressed hard to the wall, tears streamed down her face.

Without any conception of time passing, she knew only that it had. Her shoulder ached from clenching the knife. Crouching low, she held her breath and stepped in front of the door. Just the idea of looking through the peephole caused her stomach to lurch. Mustering the courage, she did what needed to be done.

No one was there. Not a soul up and down the entire hallway. At last, she exhaled. There was nowhere to hide. Wiping the sweat from her face, she backed towards Gianna's room on wobbly legs. She needed her phone to call Ash and the police. She'd managed two steps when she remembered she'd left her purse in the car!

Desperate, there was only one option. With dread in her heart, she cracked the front door. The stench hit her so hard it was like hitting a wall. There was no mistaking it. Sweeter than ethylene glycol and just as toxic, the scent was poison to her mind and miasma to her spirit. Of its own accord, her mind tripped backwards to a time of innocence and excitement. She was wearing her beautiful new prom dress and Billy was at the door to collect her. In his hand was a corsage of red and white rosebuds intertwined with sprigs of baby's breath and white ribbon. The fragrance had inundated the foyer of her parent's house.

She hadn't been able to stomach the smell of roses ever since.

Looking down, Zoey already knew what she'd find. While there was no corsage, the bouquet at her feet was enormous.

Red and white rosebuds.

Baby's breath.

White ribbon.

Her legs went weak and the world turned black...

Chapter 32

Collapsing onto Gianna's bed, Zoey buried her face in her best friend's pillow, committing her essence to memory. Eventually, her shattered mind cleared, and, setting emotion to the side for now – her brain clicked into survival mode.

If Billy had Gianna's phone, he also had her keys. There wasn't time to wonder at his game, why he chose to taunt and torment instead of taking a more direct approach. After all, he could have been laying in wait when she arrived. Rejecting that horrific thought, she sat up. He always did think he was smarter than everyone else, that he could play with human race like they were monkeys in a lab. She lifted a corner of the blind and looked down to the street. There was her car, not ten strides from the front door. Checking up and down the street, she recoiled as though she'd seen a snake.

And, in truth, she had...

This particular reptile was very large, very slimy, and very, *very* deadly. Zoey's entire body convulsed, her teeth clattering together with such force it was a miracle they didn't shatter. *Billy Pickton's car was parked three cars behind hers.* Having seen it only once – in the dark and from a distance – she couldn't be a hundred percent positive. She was positive enough, however, to stroke 'making a run for the car' off the short list of options. Those garish wheel rims were the deciding factor.

Even with her nose pressed to the glass, she couldn't see who, if anyone, was behind the wheel. The thought of Billy Pickton stalking her like prey gave her a determination she hadn't known since her competitive days. He would not best her this time. He had no idea that she'd put the pieces together, that she knew who – *and what* – he was. By now, the entire police force was probably in hot pursuit.

He figured he could just sit down there in plain sight and wait for her? Not so fast, jackass. She wasn't a dumb kid anymore. She intended to make sure the bastard rotted in jail for the rest of miserable life.

For Gianna...

But, how? She needed a plan and she needed it now. She sure as hell couldn't stay here. For all she knew, he could be in the elevator on his way up. And here she was – a sitting duck. A shiver shot up her spine. If she dwelled on such things, she'd be undone. She also couldn't dwell on what an idiot she'd been for leaving her purse in the car.

And then, out of nowhere, it came to her – her one hope of escaping undetected. She hadn't given it a thought in years. Racing down the hall to her bedroom, she forced herself to stop and think. When Gianna bought that lemon she called a car, she'd given Zoey a spare key. The question was, where did she put it? She had no idea.

Tearing open the drawer of her bedside table, she rifled through it. No key. Next, the desk. Starting at the top and working her way down, she dumped everything into a pile then went through it with a fine tooth comb. Again, no key. Tears threatened as panic rose in her throat. There was only one other possibility. If it wasn't there, she'd lost it or thrown it away. Her hands shook as she reached under the bed for the oriental box. It was where she kept mementos of her gymnastics glory days and of her dad. A thick layer of dust hid the beauty of the inlaid wood. She probably hadn't opened it since dad passed away three years ago.

Come to think of it, that was right around the time Gi bought her car...

She opened it with a prayer on her lips. And there it was, sitting right on top – a miracle on a silver platter. Clutching the key in her palm like a rosary, she formulated a plan. She still had to open the front door and edge around those nauseating flowers. From there, the route deviated from what Billy Pickton expected.

At the door to the stairwell she hesitated, imagining the worst on the other side. Holding her breath, she pushed it open. It was either that or waltz out the front door into her ardent suitors waiting arms. She crept down the stairs to the back exit and out into the tenant parking lot. The Fiat's motor turned over on the first try. *I'll never call you a lemon again, I promise!* She pulled out of the lot, her breath a series of frenetic gasps.

A block from her building, she pulled up to the stop sign that intersected her front street. Looking left and right before scooting crossing and getting the hell away from there, she saw something that kept her foot on the brake, albeit twitching with uncertainty. Billy Pickton's car was pulling away from the front of her building. It was headed down the street in the opposite direction from her.

Why was he leaving all of a sudden?

The more crucial question was where was he going? Home? She'd searched high and low for an address for both Billy Pickton and William Waters. If there was one, she hadn't found it. Or...maybe he be headed for where he'd left Gianna. With her promise to avenge her friend echoing in her head – Zoey made up her mind.

Who has the upper hand now, asshole...?

She flicked on her turn signal and took her foot off the gas. Passing her building, she missed the pair of squad cars that squealed to a stop on either side of her abandoned car...

Chapter 33

MOTHER FUCKING FUCK!

The slut must literally have flown across town. He was supposed to be waiting in Gianna's bedroom when Zoey walked in—flowers in one hand, chloroform in the other. There should have been plenty of time to get from the storage unit to her apartment, even *with* the stop to dump off some trash along the way. Now, however, he was forced to recalculate, recalibrate, and come up with another plan. Zoey's record-breaking commute combined with the accident on Ingersoll and Second made certain of that.

He'd pulled up just seconds after her, had watched her park illegally and bolt empty-handed into the building. *Odd.* Flowers in hand, he'd done a casual 'walk-by' of her vehicle. Glancing into the passenger window, he spotted her purse on the floor. Sadly, there was no telling if her phone was in it. Erring on the side of caution, he had to assume she had it with her. *Too bad.*

One thing was certain: she wasn't planning on staying long.

He did what was necessary and returned to his car. Mentally rubbing his palms together, he slid behind the wheel to await the inevitable. It was then that a jolt of foreboding sent a rare shiver down his spine. *Time was running out!* The words pulsated in his brain like a neon sign. Getting a grip on his over-active imagination, he shrugged off the premonition as a natural by-product of fatigue and exasperation.

He had all the time in the world, more than he needed, in fact.

The dipshit cops didn't have a clue who he was. None. As in zero, zippo, zilch. He, of course, was always meticulous and Gianna swore up and down she hadn't mentioned his name. To anyone. No exceptions.

He believed her. After all, a nice Catholic girl would never lie, certainly not when halfway to meeting her maker.

His dick stirred in tribute of her final moments on god's green earth. Other than that orgasmic crescendo, however, it'd been a short and rather unremarkable encounter – more a chore than anything else. The weak willed skanks of the world did so little for him, it was difficult to muster up a decent hard-on. He preferred them a little feisty – at least at first.

Gianna wasn't even wearing underwear, the useless whore. He'd had to fashion a garrotte from twine and use a screwdriver to twist it. Not nearly as satisfying as wrapping their own panties around their throats and using his own hand to govern it.

He *had* managed to get it up long enough to take some excellent photos, mind you.

Considering the sun was up by the time he was done, it was too dangerous to dump the body out in the open. Instead, he took advantage of an industrial sized garbage bin about a block over. He'd used it to dispose of a body or two over the years. Located behind a greasy spoon that tossed out bags of greasy garbage, he'd learned of the hole-in-the-wall from Darryl. When he wasn't watching porn, the dumber-than-glue manager of the storage unit would lock up the office and spend afternoons playing gin rummy with the cook.

None of the bodies he'd dumped there had ever been found. Also, in such a sparsely populated area, the chances of his being spotted were between slim to fuck all. All in all, it was the perfect final resting place for what was left of Gianna.

Parked a few cars behind Zoey's, he cracked each knuckle with a savagery usually reserved for his wife or his victims. As it turned out, the accident on Ingersoll was an omen, a sign from his guardian angel. Leaning forward, he looked up towards the whore's apartment. Exactly how did he think he was going to get her out of there, anyway? Just toss her over his shoulder like a bag of potatoes and waltz out the front door in broad daylight? Yeah. Pretty fucking stupid.

He'd gotten overexcited, what with a key to her house in his hot little hand.

With victory so close he could literally reach out and snatch it, he needed to keep his cool more than ever. He'd sacrificed much for this one slut, he would not be denied. His intent was to squeeze every drop of well-deserved pleasure from her body, her mind, and her spirit.

With that ultimate objective in mind, the more prudent plan had been to place the roses at her door and return to his car to await her return. After discovering his thoughtful gift, she was sure to come reeling from the building and straight into his clutches. He'd have her bundled into his car in less time than it took to blink.

And, yet, it was twenty minutes later and she still hadn't emerged. *Was it possible she'd forgotten him?* He'd never considered the possibility. Pressure began to build in his head, a precursor to a rage he didn't care to control. He couldn't sit here much longer, especially with a bottle of chloroform and a rag at his side. Even a cow as stupid as Zoey would smell a rat after finding the apartment empty.

At best, she'd have called her beefhead boyfriend. At

worst, the cops.

MOTHER FUCKING FUCK!

Pulling away from the curb, he was sure a cranial blood vessel was about to burst. Timing was of the essence and he'd fucked up royally. While he wasn't vain enough to believe himself invincible, he did have the IQ of a genius and the cunning of a fox. For reassurance, he grasped his flaccid dick through his pants and squeezed so hard that the searing pressure in his head relocated to his scrotum.

Ahhh...much better.

With a clearer head, he reasoned that he'd waited this long, one more day wouldn't kill him. In fact, after the all-nighter he'd pulled? A little down time was starting to sound like a damn good idea. He wasn't as young as he once was. Optimism reinstated, he tuned into some good old-fashioned rock'n'roll. There were two things he needed: a workable plan and a nap. Figuring the former would come to him as he indulged in the latter, he headed home for some shut-eye.

He noticed the red and white Fiat as he turned right onto Jackson. Two cars behind him, the Italian buggy was as out of place as a puck at a football game. Yet, considering there weren't that many around, he was sure he'd seen it before.

Somewhere...

It was still behind him at the Brookside Boulevard lights. Ruminating at the red, it hit him like bullet to the brain: *It was Gianna's car!* He'd glimpsed it briefly on their first date a couple months back. Having hooked up on social media, she thought it prudent to meet on neutral ground. *A girl can never be too careful, si bello?* He chuckled, remembering her ill-fated words. After that, he'd always picked her up. There was only one explanation for the dead woman's car to be following him.

Zoey was behind the wheel!

Aside from the question of how she'd recognized *his* car, the rest made perfect sense. No wonder she hadn't bolted out the front door as he'd expected. The sneaky whore thought she could outwit him and had bolted out the back instead. Taking a left, a wide smile spread across his face. He could almost feel depravity and malice dripping from the corners. She didn't realize she was playing cat and mouse with a rabid jackal.

Not as young as he once was? Needed a little down time?

Not any more.

Suddenly, he felt as potent as an eighteen year old on his way to pick up his date for the prom...

Chapter 34

Ash was beside himself. Pacing like a caged animal before Percy O'Malley's desk, he could still feel the heat of Zoey's little hands tugging at his wrist. The trust emanating from her bottomless green eyes had been absolute. Her words echoed in his head: *I love you too...I love you too...I love you too...*

The Chief was juggling three phone lines at once. Thanks to Zoey's game-changing discoveries, he had more than enough probable cause for a search warrant to be served on the home of William Waters a.k.a. Billy Pickton. He requested a second for the suspect's offices on Chancellor Avenue. Aside from the warrants, he wanted to know everything there was to know about the man—background, marital status, vehicles, travel destinations, if he owned any other properties—everything. He was most interested in his whereabouts the night Gianna disappeared and on the dates of the murders.

The murders they knew of, that is. They'd begun to suspect there might be more...

After learning he'd played cards and shot the shit with a psychopath, Percy wasn't as shocked as Ash expected.

"They don't call me 'The Nose' for nothing, my friend. You think I was shooting the shit with that piece of fruitcake? It's my nature to collect intel on folks that give me the willies, and, that guy gave me a serious case of 'em. But, with nothing except the slime factor and a gut feeling, why would I mention it? If you recall, he was there as your guest."

Ash recalled only too well. Nobody could have guessed

that this particular slimeball was a serial killer with an obsession for gymnasts. *No, not gymnasts.* Gymnast, singular. More than ever, he believed the sick fuck's obsession began and ended with Zoey. *His Zoey.* What she might be going through right now did not bear thinking about. If he dwelled on it, he'd be finished. Done in. A blithering half-wit.

He couldn't allow that. He intended to have a moment or two alone with the sick son of a bitch...

The office was bustling. With a confirmed serial killer running rampant, the FBI was getting involved. A steady stream of agents, detectives, uniformed officers and other personnel came and went. Someone offered Ash a bottle of water which he accepted with a grateful nod and a shaking hand. Gulping it down, every swallow sounded like a gun going off in his head. His throat remained Mojave Desert dry.

With a conscious effort, he released the death grip on his phone, wishing instead it were the neck of William Waters, a.k.a. Billy Pickton. If that were the case, he'd snap it like a toothpick and not break a sweat.

With nothing better to do, he punched redial. He already knew it wouldn't end well, but was compelled to try. Zoey's phone rang until her voice mail kicked in. Thanks to the desperate stream of messages he'd already left, her mailbox was full. As it was half a dozen calls ago. He listened to every word of her sweet voice: *Hi, this is Zoey. I'll get back to you as soon as I can. Promise!*

Minutes passed second by torturous second whereas hours seemed to fly. The anguish was such that his very soul ached. He should never have left her alone. Yet, she'd been in no shape to come with him and he'd had no choice but to go. The gym had been a mad house. He'd decided to close it, at least for the day. Parents were notified. They arrived en mass, a frenzied stampede of panic and fear. Last to arrive was Mercedes, oblivious to everything and everyone other than herself. Flouncing past the melee, she all but spat at him, breath fetid with hostility.

"I had to cancel my appointment with Ricardo. I've been waiting months to see him, and now? I'm dead to him. He'll never book me again."

Dead to him? Had she really said that? She never failed to amaze. He was disinclined to bother with a filter.

"Would you rather be dead to 'Ricardo', Mercedes—or just plain dead? You choose. If you decide to stay, I'll be happy to put Cherish on a plane without you and save a few bucks."

He shouldn't have, but there was no taking it back. Hatred distorted her face. For a woman who dedicated her life to looking younger, she wasn't doing a very good job. Her features were pinched and mottled, her pupils shards of glacial ice. He wouldn't have been surprised if her hair transformed into hissing serpents and he was rendered a pillar of salt. The sound that came out of her was something between a squawk and a hiss.

Apparently, when all else failed, her new fallback plan was to attack Zoey.

"This is all because of your new slut, isn't it? She must be as fucked up as you are!"

He'd turned his back on her then. There were important things to take care of.

"Sit down and conserve your energy, boy. You're not helping anything by wearing a track in my hardwood."

Percy's booming voice brought him out of his own head.

His friend's attempt to lighten the mood fell flat and everyone in the room knew it. Even so, Ash threw himself into a chair. Adrenalin rocketed through his veins at breakneck speed. In a cold sweat, it felt as if he were processing the world from under water. His nervous system was ready for a fight or a flight – one or the other. Sitting on his ass doing sweet fuck all was not an available option.

He knew something was terribly wrong the moment he'd heard Zoey's message. *Gianna was at home, safe and sound?* It made no sense, no sense at all. He was afraid to think about who'd been texting her, but it wasn't Gianna. Zoey would have figured it out had she only stopped to think. Her eagerness to believe her girlfriend was okay had overridden her common sense.

"Abandoned? In the loading zone, you say? Flowers?"

The dismay in the Chief's voice transcended the professional. Jerking his head up, Percy's compassion-filled eyes pierced his own. Ash's head nearly spun off its axis. Even if his heart weren't wedged into his throat, he wouldn't dare interrupt the urgent call. They needed every single piece of information if they were to save Zoey. Thankfully, his friend's compassion did not get in the way of his getting shit done.

"Have the car towed to the compound. Find out where the flowers came from, who paid for them and how. We need fingerprints, as well. I want any and all video from the apartment, from every angle. Don't forget to check the cross streets. I want to know where she went and with whom."

Ash sat numb, reckoning the horrific meaning of the call when another was buzzed through. This time, Percy's voice dropped to a calming whisper. He motioned with his hand to the closest FBI agent, then pointed to the receiver.

"Yes, this is Chief O'Malley. How can I help you Mrs. Waters?..."

Chapter 35

She was adorable, the way she thought she was in control.

Having made an about-face, he headed straight for the east side of town, Zoey in hot pursuit. He couldn't shake the whore if he tried. She was the perfect tail, pardon the pun. Cackling at his hilarity, he managed to pat himself on the back while keeping both hands on the wheel. Thanks to his quick thinking and versatility, he'd concocted a plan that was nothing short of brilliant. Although more discreet than the fiasco that had played out at her apartment, it was still fraught with peril. Shrugging his shoulders, he checked the side-view mirror. Sometimes in life, the reward outweighed the risk. In this case, it was a no-brainer.

Speaking of no-brainers, there she was, three cars back, a cross between an inept *James Bond* and an obedient puppy. He'd been wrong about her phone. Clearly, she did not have it on her. If she did, he'd have been swarmed by cops by now. The defenseless bitch had no idea she was being led to the slaughter.

But, first, he had a nice juicy bone for her...

His dick began dancing the moment he realized he was being followed – and by whom. Now, it was a solid mass of throbbing lust demanding gratification. Incredibly, he'd just tossed two jism filled condoms into the trash alongside Gianna's rotting body. A testament to masculinity and good, clean living, he stroked the turgid column through his pants, soothing it like a fussy baby. When he spoke, his voice wavered with pride.

"Our patience has paid off, my impassioned friend. No

more condoms for you."

The next few hours would mark the culmination of his fantasies. His and Zoey's second date would end a decade's worth of perseverance and self-sacrifice. He intended to milk the cow dry, then leave the carcass for the vultures. From there, he was dust in the wind, off to Zagreb surrounded by his loving family.

Accelerating down Eighth, he passed Petunia and turned onto Daffodil, a dilapidated dead end which led straight to his dreams. Other than a row of shabby residences, many of which were boarded up—the only structure of note was the storage facility at the far end. While an eight foot fence ran the length of it, the peaked roofs towered above it, casting a jagged shadow over the entire street. He needed to get there and be out of sight when she turned. It would be tight. He rocketed down the deserted street, pulled a quick right, and cut the engine.

If his luck held, Darryl the moron manager was either AWOL or glued to some flick, whacking off.

Speaking of whacking off, he looked forward to having Zoey do it for him. Imagining her little hand working the shaft of his dick did much for his libido but little for his focus. Still, he couldn't help but wonder how many twists of the garrotte would be required before she eagerly complied. He looked forward to finding out. As did his cohort in crime, if the party going on in his tighty whities was any indication.

In preparation, he reached across the seat and cracked open the passenger door. If things went according to plan, he would soon have his hands full – too full to manage even that simple task. Uncapping the chloroform and folding the rag into a neat square, he exited the vehicle to peer through the slats of the fence.

The participants of note were on board. All systems were go. The only unknown was whether the worthless whore would cooperate...

* * * * *

Perspiration poured down Zoey's face, stinging her eyes. Her hair was glued to the back of her neck, as were the clothes to her body. The stench of tension and plain old-fashioned fear clung to her every gasping breath. Her shoulder was killing her.

After all that, she'd lost him.

Undecided as to whether she was devastated or relieved, she forced one hand from the wheel and shook the ache from its petrified joints. She repeated the action with the other claw-like appendage. She was positive he'd turned down Petunia, but there was no sign of him. About to give up and turn back, she noticed the street sign for Daffodil Drive. It was the last street before an open field criss-crossed with railway tracks.

She'd come this far, she might as well explore all avenues. Not even cracking a smile at the pun, she pulled the steering wheel hard, mind made up. If possible, Daffodil was even more decrepit than its predecessor. A sorry succession of broken down, cookie-cutter houses, its name was the sole bloom on the block. She crawled down the length of it, head swivelling left and right. Again, she came up empty. Billy Pickton had managed to give her the slip.

She wondered when he'd realized he was being tailed.

Looking up, she eyeballed the storage facility looming

before her. Hope blossomed in her chest. There must be an office in there, and in that office – there would be a telephone. With her sleeve, she mopped the sweat from her brow, catching it just before it dripped into her eyes. Ash must be worried sick. The thought punctured her heart. Pulling up alongside the fence, she turned off the engine. Exhaling so hard her cheeks puffed, she took a moment to collect herself.

The rear-view mirror told an ugly tale. Ashen, her jaw was clenched so hard, veins throbbed in both temples. Her hands shook as she pushed damp curls off her face and tucked them behind her ears. Stepping out of the Fiat, she tested rubbery legs. Confident she could support herself, she started up the gravel drive. There was a sign about thirty yard to the left and she headed towards it.

The attack came out of nowhere, knocking the breath from her lungs.

She wanted to scream, wanted to with the whole of her being, but the forearm pressing against her Adam's apple forbade it. There was no time to think, only to react. Gripped with a terror she'd never imagined, Zoey twisted and kicked for all she was worth. She might have given him a run for his money, too, if his other hand hadn't come into play.

It covered her nose and mouth, pressing down hard. A sharp antiseptic smell assailed her nostrils. Immediately, she felt woozy. As her ears rang and her body tingled, the fight drained from her. Just before the world turned to black, Billy Pickton whispered into her ear.

"At last...we meet again..."

Chapter 36

You'd never guess a five year old lived here. There wasn't a bicycle, a wagon, a chalk drawing – nothing. The curbside appeal of the sprawling Victorian gingerbread house was pristine. While it appeared Stepford perfect, Ash's skin began to crawl the moment he, Chief O'Malley, two detectives, and four uniformed officers set foot on the Waters' cheery veranda.

Precious hours had passed since he'd arrived home to find Zoey gone. Since he'd listened to her chilling message and left dozens in return. Since he'd almost blown a gasket in Percy O'Malley's office. Even at their most efficient, the wheels of justice turned slowly. Red tape hobbled productivity at every turn.

Percy had made him promise to not say a word. If he could manage that, he'd be allowed to sit in on Irina Waters' interview. He'd crossed his heart, Boy Scout earnest. Whether or not he was going to keep that promise remained to be seen. With Zoey in mortal danger, he was willing to do or say just about anything to get her back.

Billy Pickton's wife welcomed them, if you could call it that. Cracking the door open a fraction of an inch, she peered out at them. Other than one eyeball—pale blue, desolate, and dilated with what appeared to be fear—he could see little of the suspected serial killer's spouse. First and foremost, she was going to have to convince him that she wasn't her hubby's partner in crime. Despite what the FBI profiler said, he couldn't fathom she'd known nothing of his proclivities for all these years.

It was only after Percy flashed his badge that she stepped away from the door, leaving it for the Chief to push open. One look at the broken woman huddled in the foyer erased any notion of her involvement. A shadow of her former self, she looked nothing like the photo on her immigration application. Just six years ago, Irina was a young, vibrant woman with shining blonde locks, a cute button nose, and a sparkle in her eye.

Today, she was unrecognizable. Hunched into what could only be described as an upright fetal position, her bony arms clung to protuberant ribs. Either she was afflicted with early onset osteoporosis, or she lived in a perpetual state of terror. When she raised her head, the answer was written all over her face. One eye was swollen completely shut. Rimmed in swatches of black and blue and orange and yellow, it was obvious her face served double duty as a punching bag. Her nose resembled that of a second-rate boxer, flattened and crooked from repeated pummeling. Her once long, lustrous hair was chopped, in some spots to the scalp—as was the hair of the child peeking at them from behind her mother's skirt.

As was the hair of the three known victims...

Under other circumstances, Ash might have felt something for their appalling plight. Compassion. Disgust. Rage. All of the above. Under the current circumstances, however, he had to restrain himself from screaming at the woman to hurry the fuck up and tell them what they needed to know. Didn't she understand that a single second could mean the difference between life and death for his babygirl?

When she offered them lemonade, he wanted to throttle her himself. The quaver in her voice left him cold.

The detectives and uniformed cops fanned out, scouring

the house for evidence. He, the Chief, and their hostess settled into the Stepford-style living room for a 'chat'. If there was a single mote of dust in the entire residence, he'd not seen it. After twenty seconds in an ill-fitting but uber-stylish armchair, Ash had a better idea. Opening the oppressive curtains, he paced the length of the picture window.

A forensics van was just pulling up behind the squad cars. There were fingerprints to lift. Tire treads to photograph. DNA to collect. Hovering at her mother's shoulder, the child stared first at him and then out the window, slack-jawed. Looking around, he noticed that every window covering in the house was made of black-out material and pulled closed. The place was gloomier than a tomb. Both mother and child were as pale as vampires. When he turned back, however, only the mother remained. The child had vanished, as silent as a mouse.

"He get worse. Every day he get worse. I afraid. I afraid he kill us."

Her accent was thick. It was obvious she struggled to find the words.

"I understand, Mrs. Waters. You were right to call. You mentioned you found something disturbing?"

"Da."

Uncrossing her arms, she reached into the pocket of her shapeless shift. Holding his breath, Ash waited for her to pull out the magic key that would crack open the case and save Zoey's life. Instead, she hesitated.

"I saw news. You."

She nodded in Percy's direction, but did not attempt to make eye contact.

"You call my husband is killer. Raper of woman. I

173

supposed to not use phone. I phone what you call 'tip line'."

Having spoken her piece, she pulled her hand from her pocket and extended her arm as far as it would go. Disgust was written all over her face, punctuated by shame. Hanging from between her thumb and forefinger was an enormous pair of women's underwear. Once cute, the heart-shaped smiley faces covering them were now macabre reminders of the fate of its owner. Ash thought he was going to throw up.

"On floor in garage. Next to car."

Without missing a beat, Percy whipped out his phone and took a picture of the panties while still in Irina Waters' possession. Removing a plastic bag from his jacket pocket, he used a pen to relieve her of them. On closer examination, they weren't enormous at all – they were stretched. Streaks of what looked like blood were intermingled with the hearts. Remembering the ligature marks found around the women's necks, Ash sat down before his legs gave out.

Zoey!

The consummate professional, Chief O'Malley didn't blink an eye as he fished the panties into the plastic bag and tucked them away. Excusing himself, he pulled one of the detectives into another room. Ash was left alone with his closest link to Zoey. Irina Waters' husband already had – or was about to – perpetrate unspeakable acts on the woman he loved. As much as he wished it otherwise, he knew it deep in his soul. The lunatic's thirst for torturing and killing knew no bounds and Zoey was the cherry on the half-baked cake of his madness. Where Ash was bouncing around like an adrenaline-fuelled basket case, Irina sat stoically, avoiding eye-contact at all costs.

In the twenty minutes it took for the Chief to return, he'd

exhausted every last ounce of restraint he possessed. Percy patted his shoulder before taking his seat and resuming the interview.

"We've got men at his offices on Chancellor, ma'am. Do you know of any other properties or businesses he might frequent? Favorite hangouts? Friends? Anything?"

The spouse of a serial killer shook her head.

"I sorry. I yim not familiar with this chane cellor?"

Turning away in disgust, Ash stared out the window, heart sinking. As an alternative to thinking, he watched as a red and white Fiat cruised past the house and the sidewalk full of inquisitive neighbors. He'd always been interested in foreign cars, and this one was going slow enough to make out every detail. The driver, slouched in his seat, looked more than a little uncomfortable. Either it belonged to his girlfriend or it was an odd choice of vehicle for such a large man.

Beside him, Percy stood to leave. Reluctantly, Ash tuned back into reality.

"We're going to take you and your daughter into protective custody, ma'am. Officer Jenkins will go with you to collect a few things."

"Ana? *Ana?*"

Alarmed, the mother's voice went up an octave. Ash looked around. The little girl who'd slipped away from her mother's side nearly an hour ago had still not returned...

Chapter 37

She was weightless, floating in a pea-soupy haze. At the same time, she was immobilized under a weight so crushing, she struggled to draw air. She needed to run, to swim, to fly, and, yet, her limbs hung useless, the only sign of life a random spasm. From off in the distance, an annoying snipping sound distracted her. Unable to place it, she redoubled her efforts to move. Still, to no avail.

The weight was becoming unbearable, her limbs refused to cooperate, and...the snipping was getting louder. Closer...

Afraid, she called out to Ash and he was there, filling the nooks and crannies of her mind. She so wanted to take his face into her hands, but, alas, was unable. Instead, she memorized every curve, every crevice, every pore. The love that radiated from his eyes was her bulwark. She clung to it with all her strength, trusting in it to keep her safe.

"How's your shoulder, babygirl?"

What an odd question for him to ask. And, at such an odd time, as well. While she wasn't sure exactly what 'time' it was, it seemed odd nonetheless. Why was he concerned about her shoulder? Could he intuit the throbbing pain?

Someone called her name, but, it wasn't her beloved. Vaguely, she recognized the voice. Right now, however, she had other things to worry about than putting a name to it. The weight on her chest was becoming unbearable. The snipping sound was so close, it was as though it were inside her head. Worst of all, Ash's face was distorting before her eyes.

"Ash! Please...please, don't leave me!"

"I love you Zoey Benton..."

His features became wisps of smoke before evaporating into nothingness. The anguish in her heart was intolerable. The only bright spot was that her legs were beginning to respond to her brain's commands.

"WAKE UP, WHORE!"

Pain brought her fully awake, the last vestiges of sweet oblivion snatched away by a single vicious blow. Her head snapped sideways with the impact, eyes flying open. Her jaw wasn't dislocated, but it was definitely out of kilter.

"Well, good morning! I can't tell you how wonderful it is to see you. It's been far too long, wouldn't you agree?"

The horror of reality superceded her worst nightmare by a landslide. Naked, she was flat on her back looking up at the ceiling of a small, windowless room. Her jagged breath sounded oddly muffled. The floor, the walls, and even the ceiling were wrapped in some black, spongy looking material. Other than a table and chair in one corner, the room was devoid of furniture.

Her arms were bound behind her, hands positioned in such a way that they cupped her own buttocks. Her only cushion was the black, not-as-spongy-as-it-looked overlay. Her bad shoulder throbbed in time with her jaw and her skull.

As grim as it was, it got worse.

"I've taken the liberty of fixing your hair. I must say it was a rat's nest."

A naked psychopath straddled her chest, a malevolent grin on his face. The crazy in Billy Pickton's eyes was as terrifying as his state of undress. Cold and flat as a lizard's, they sparkled feverishly. While his entire body was shaven clean, he was nonetheless covered in hair. Long, brown, and kinky, it took her stunned brain a moment to comprehend that it was *hers*. The disconcerting snipping sounds she thought she'd imagined were no longer a mystery.

The horror of having her hair hacked off left her breathless. From what she could tell, there wasn't a single strand left on her head that was longer than half an inch. Her mind snapped into preservation mode. The world went out of kilter as she floated outside of herself.

From that safe sanctuary, she observed his rock-hard penis vibrating between her breasts, its slimy tip oozing. A pool of white semen coagulated in the chasm. If the sight wasn't revolting enough, there was no evading the stench. Both it and he stunk of acrid perspiration and stale sex. Zoey sobbed, thinking of her best friend. Her name formed on her dry, cracked lips.

"Gianna..."

This time she saw the blow coming. This time, the fist was closed. Helpless to avoid it, all she could do was brace for the impact. Abject terror roiled in her stomach and blasted up the back of her throat. Before she could vomit, Billy Pickton, once considered the smartest and most handsome boy in school—punched her square in the face. She managed to turn her head at the last second, but it still caught the corner of her eye with the force of a hammer.

Pain ricocheted to her brain, where it came face to face with her own mortality. Vomit pumped from between her lips, slid down her cheek, into her ear, and finally, onto the corrugated floor. She was going to die here, bound naked in a pool of her own vomit. Like Gianna. Like Jersey. Like who knew how many others.

His voice was gleeful. The sick son of a bitch was enjoying himself.

"Funny you should mention her name. When I was choking the last breath from her lungs—she mentioned yours, as well."

Sobbing, Zoey understood this was her last day on

earth...

Chapter 38

"Give us a nice smile now, babycakes. Those bruises together with the terror on your whorish face will get me off long after you're not around to do so."

"I won't. You might as well kill me now."

She meant it, too. If the outcome was a forgone conclusion, she wasn't about to play his sadistic games. His demented laughter dismantled her conviction. If possible, her blood ran colder than it already was. Shards of ice raced through her veins. It was only a matter of time until one pierced her heart. In truth, she looked forward to it.

Rather that – than this hell on earth...

"Still feisty, I see? You won't be for long, that I can promise."

The whacko that had ruined her life a decade ago and was now intent on ending it cackled with glee.

"Speaking of not being feisty for long, I appreciate your wearing a nice sturdy pair of underwear, unlike your girlfriend, who didn't wear any, scrawny cow that she was."

That's when she learned the full extent of Billy Pickton's madness. His hand shot out. Zoey flinched. Bones were sure to break if he struck her a third time. Instead, he reached for something near her throat. When he began to twist it, she realized it wasn't 'near' her throat – *it was around it.*

Her underwear!?

There was no time for shock. No time for horror. The oxygen to her brain was cut off with a single violent jerk. Immediately, she was in survival mode, fighting for her life. Legs flailing, her eyeballs bulged from their sockets. Spots danced before them as white lights exploded behind. She couldn't draw air, not a single molecule. She needed...needed to tear it away, needed to fight... Instinctively, she struggled to free her arms of their restraints. They dug gouges into her wrists but didn't budge. It wasn't long before her legs stopped flailing and the light behind her eyes began to fade. When her bladder voided, she reconciled herself to joining dad, Hal, and Gianna.

And, then—it stopped.

She sucked in precious oxygen through a burning airway the size of a dime. Gasping and sputtering, tears poured down her face. Every nerve ending was on fire. Her broken voice didn't qualify as a croak.

"Please...no more..."

"Oh, yes, much more, I promise. You're going to die with your panties imbedded in your throat, but, not quite yet. I have so many surprises planned, it's really quite exciting. This is the tenth anniversary of our first date. How would it look if I stinted on such a meaningful occasion?"

She had to know.

"But...why?"

"But, why not? It pleases me, that's reason enough. I fantasize about raping, hurting, humiliating. *You*, in particular. Yes, it all begins and ends with you – quite an honor for such a useless whore. Back then, you were so talented, so confident. *Too* talented. *Too* confident. I was so looking forward to putting you in your place. I took the responsibility seriously, planned meticulously. It was the tiniest miscalculation that brings us here today."

"Please...I'm sorry..."

She wasn't able to assimilate his words. They struck her

eardrums, but her brain was having none of it. Suddenly, she wanted to sleep. Billy Pickton had other plans.

"Enough chit chat, bitch. I believe I asked you to do something?"

He picked up his camera, slung it around his neck, made some adjustments – and grinned. It was surreal, deranged. Billy Pickton was as excited as a kid in a candy store, with one hand on his camera and the other working his cock. She thought of Ash and the beautiful life they could have had together. New tears stung her eyes, one of which had swollen shut.

It felt like a butcher knife was imbedded in her heart, another in her skull. Nonetheless, she'd do anything – *anything*—to not endure that agony again.

Peeling her lips away from her teeth, she stretched them into a macabre smile.

"That's more like it. I hate having to ask twice."

The camera clicked then clicked again, the flash blinding.

"Speaking of pictures, I have a few I took of Gianna that I'm *dying* to share with you."

Nooo...

A ragged sob tore from her ragged throat, the prospect unimaginable. *What kind of monster could inflict such torture?* She was his toy, a rat in a maze of his construction, nothing resembling a human being. It was too grotesque to fathom. Whimpering, Zoey's throbbing jaw worked but no words formed. With his genitals glued to her chest, Billy Pickton leaned over to rummage through a bag she hadn't noticed.

"Ahhh, this one's lovely, don't you agree? We had fun, despite the fact I couldn't get it up for a nice ass-fucking. As you can see, that's not going to be a problem where you're concerned."

His words were incomprehensible, his maniacal laughter terrifying. Zoey refused to look, squeezing her one good eye shut. His voice was low, flat, terrifying.

"Open your fucking eyes. Consider this your final warning."

Every fiber of her being screamed no. Her mind screamed no. And, yet, with shame in her heart, Zoey opened her eyes.

What she saw drove her to the brink. Turning her head to the side, she heaved and vomited again, swallowing back the acrid remains. A savage blow to her left breast barely registered in her tormented mind. Nonetheless, she turned back to face the grisly remains of her best friend. Gianna was unrecognizable. She laid naked and spread-eagled, her slender body covered in cuts and bruises. Her hair had been chopped, leaving uneven tufts where glorious, waist-length tresses used to fall. Purple lacerations encircled her throat. As horrific as it was, the worst was her eyes. Open and lifeless, they testified to the abominations she'd endured.

Heartsick for her friend, Zoey saw her future. The words slipped out before she could stop them.

"You're insane..."

When his hand shot out again, every muscle in her body contracted in terror. She opened her mouth to scream, but it was too late. Her airway was blocked, utterly and completely. Once again, she was fighting for her life, a two hundred pound beast weighing her down. Her ears rang once. Then again and again. Zoey went limp, too weak to fight. When the pressure was released, she gulped down air, not sure she wasn't sorry to still be alive. Her entire body was in spasm. Luckily, the level of fear she'd attained numbed all pain. As oxygen returned to her brain, so did some awareness of what was going on around her.

The weight was gone from her chest. She could hear his vile voice. What she thought was ringing in her ears had been Billy Pickton's phone.

"Why are you calling me?"

The pause was miniscule.

"What do you mean goodbye? Yeah, yeah, I love you too. Now, what does goodbye mean?"

Under different circumstances, the idea of him loving another human would be laughable. Right now, however, all she wanted to do was go to sleep and never wake up.

"Hello?...Hello?...What the...?"

"MOTHER FUCKING FUCK!"

Whatever was happening, he was major league pissed. He paced back and forth, holding his penis and muttering to himself in two different voices. It was as if he were holding a conversation with his genitals. Even if she were able, she wouldn't raise an eyebrow. To Zoey's shredded mind, it didn't seem the least bit odd. She drifted in and out of reality, moaning with every rasping breath. She was almost asleep when she felt her legs being lifted like an infant about to have its diaper changed. Her heart rate went through the roof.

"Spread open those god damned ass cheeks and do it now!"

This is it. The end. The 'ass-fucking' Gianna had managed to escape before losing her life. There was no escape for Zoey. Now she understood why her hands were bound palm-down. *But...why...why was he dressed?* She didn't dare hesitate. Dead inside, she pulled her butt-cheeks wide.

"This time, the dosage is more than enough."

And, with that, he shoved something into her anal cavity and released her legs. She curled into a ball on her side, pulled her knees into the fetal position, and waited to die. Somewhere, a door opened. The last thing she heard was Billy Pickford's cruel voice.

"The whore'll be out for hours..."

Chapter 39

Stuffed behind the wheel of Gianna's Fiat, he was hard-pressed to stay within the speed limit. The thought of being stopped for speeding in a dead woman's car helped considerably. Under the circumstances, he felt the Fiat was a better choice than his Lincoln. Covert trumped overt every time, especially when he didn't know what the fuck was going on. He had to get it off the street, in any case.

He'd left his car in the storage unit and walked out. If dumb Darryl proved inquisitive, he had a bullshit story ready to go. It wasn't necessary. The office was closed. No doubt, the absentee manager was down the street, getting paid to play cards with his buddy.

Ana never called in the middle of the day. Never. She knew better, had learned the hard way. He wasn't pissed, he was seething with murderous rage. But, he was also perplexed. Why *had* she called? And, why was she whispering? *Bye-bye daddy. I love you daddy. Bye-bye.* Had Irina put her up to it? She'd been pushing her luck lately, making eye contact and asking questions as if she thought she had rights.

Was the cunt taunting him? She couldn't even call a cab, never mind have the wherewithal to leave him. The idea was too preposterous to entertain. On the other hand, the call was too far out of the ordinary to let slide. He wouldn't be able to enjoy himself until it was settled. And, if there was one thing he wanted, it was to enjoy the living shit out of his long overdue rendezvous with Zoey Benton. She'd been his sole focus for a decade. Everything else, including his success as a photographer, was motivated by that singular obsession.

He would put his house in order and hurry back to their reunion. She'd still be out cold. Maybe he'd curl up beside her and catch a few Z's.

The moment he turned onto his street, however, he realized he was in trouble. His driveway was bumper-to-bumper with cop cars, both marked and unmarked. There were so many they spilled out onto the street. A white forensics van stood open, hair-netted and slipper-footed investigators traipsing back and forth with their findings. Nosy neighbors lined the streets, gaping and gossiping.

He needed to get the fuck out of there. But, pulling a three-point U-y in the middle of a residential street was sure to draw unwanted attention. On the other hand, if he didn't, someone was sure to recognize his car.

That's when he remembered that he wasn't in his car, he was in Gianna's. In a neighborhood crammed with Porsches and Lexuses, nobody was going to give a piece of shit Fiat a second glance. Crouching even lower in the seat, he pulled his shoulders up to his ears. He drove by his own house at a crawl, just another curious gawker.

Back on Brookside Boulevard, his head exploded. Rage consumed him. *What the fuck was going on?* If Irina was fed up with his escalating violence, that was one thing. But, what he saw back there sure as shit wasn't your standard, garden variety domestic abuse call. That was a full-on investigation.

It wasn't possible. He'd crossed every motherfucking T, dotted every cocksucking I. Irina didn't know shit, he was positive of that. Whatever was going on, one thing was certain: They had no idea about the storage unit. He'd been meticulous, going through so many dummy corporations and aliases that the trail was convoluted to the point of being untraceable. It was a dead end, literally and figuratively.

Nonetheless, it was time for him to get the hell out of Dodge. Screw the bitch and the kid. He'd use one of his many passports and disappear forever, leaving those keystone cops scratching their doltish heads. He might have to cut short his time with Zoey., but, not by much. He hadn't come this far for nothing. He would have his just rewards, that was set in stone.

By the time he turned onto Daffodil, calm and confidence was restored. By losing the dead weight of his wife and kid, Plan B was even better than Plan A. The morons back at the house had no idea the level of intelligence they were dealing with. He would have his cake and eat it too. Backing the Fiat into the storage unit, he parked it next to the Lincoln. Reaching into the Lincoln's passenger side, he removed the Glock from the glove compartment. One could never be too careful...

The simple act of unlocking the door to his 'playroom' got his cock so hard, it hurt. It was time to finish what was started a decade ago...

Chapter 40

Hamstrung, there was nothing for Ash to do but sit. Sit and wait. Sit and hope for a break. Sit and pray for a miracle.

In other words—sit and lose his fucking mind!

Every cop on the force was out searching for this asshole and, still – not a whiff. While authorities rushed to compare fingerprints and DNA collected at the Waters' residence to any found on the victims, his Zoey was still in the clutches of a psychopath. A psychopath who took his pleasure from torturing and killing women. The thought made him heave.

They'd just left the bastard's house. In the passenger seat of Percy's unmarked vehicle, helplessness was joined by hopelessness. The weight was crushing. He was a man of action— strong and capable. Yet, when Zoey needed him most, there wasn't a fucking thing he could do to help her. His friend's voice barely cracked through the solid wall of misery engulfing him.

"Ash. I know it's hard, but try to stay positive. We're going to find him. I promise you that."

Ash nodded, not trusting his voice. He believed Percy would find him. The question was: *would he find him in time?* With a hundred thousand dollar reward up for grabs, tips were pouring in. Yet, there were only X-number of resources available to run them down and only X-number of hours in the day to do so.

So far, they'd gotten nowhere. The general consensus was that he was holed up somewhere off the grid. Either that, or he'd already skipped town. His wife told them he travelled often for business. There was an APB out on the man and a

BOLO issued for his '95 Lincoln.

Still, nothing...

The Chief had left directions for the most promising tips be redirected to him. Maybe he was fooling himself, but he'd swear he could hear Zoey calling for him. In his mind's eye, he could see her reaching for him. She was still alive, he felt it. He vowed to not sleep, eat, shit, or leave Percy O'Malley's side until they found her.

When Percy's cell phone rang, Ash nearly shed his skin. He needed to get ahold of himself. At this rate, he'd be dead of a coronary before the day was out. No doubt, it was just another tip that led nowhere.

"The East Side Eatery? What time was that, did you say? Uh-huh. Uh-huh. Excellent. Keep him there, we're on our way."

Was that excitement he heard in the stoic Chief's voice? Ash struggled to contain the nugget of hope in his chest. He'd have to wait to find out. Percy held a forefinger up in his direction, a signal to hold his questions. Once he'd alerted the detectives and pulled a U-y, he gave him his full attention. Ash's question was now a choked statement of fact.

"They found a body."

He gripped the arm rest so hard, veins throbbed in his temples. His testicles constricted, retracting into his body. If it was Zoey, he couldn't be held responsible for his actions.

"Yes. In a garbage bin behind a restaurant. It's at the same end of town where the body was found in the landfill. Remote. Low traffic. It sounds credible. Ash, I know what you're thinking..."

Not to mention the terror that must be written all over his clammy face...

"It's not Zoey, Ash. The timeline's not right. A homeless man saw the body being dumped this morning. It was too early for it to be Zoey. Now, buck up. It's somewhere to start..."

* * * * *

To call the East Side Eatery a restaurant would be like calling a hunk of shit a diamond. Why the Health Department hadn't condemned the dump was a mystery that evoked images of mafia-style payoffs. A stop for truckers punchy from driving and hungry enough to eat excrement, the cloying stench of fryer oil hung heavy in the air. Every surface was slick with it. Ash's stomach heaved in revolt.

At this hour, the place was pretty much empty. What looked to be a strung out drug addict sat in the closest booth, guzzling chocolate milk and scarfing down pie. Two other men sat on stools at the counter, only one of whom was eating. The other was playing cards with the cook, a caricature straight out of central casting. The mile-high chef's hat balanced on his head was every shade of filthy.

Jack, the owner, had met them at the door. Shaking his hand as if it were clean, Percy flashed his badge and introduced himself. He was eager to talk to the person who'd discovered the body. Crews were already working to remove it from the bin out back. The entire alley was roped off as a crime scene.

Putting the pieces together, there was only one conclusion. The girl thrown away like trash that morning was Gianna Ricci—Zoey's oldest and dearest friend. For the umpteenth time, Ash swallowed back the nausea that threatened.

Any hope he'd had left dissolved when the owner pointed them in the direction of the booth. The guy didn't look like he knew his own name.

"Gus? Gus Sandoval?"

Gus Sandoval looked up, chewing for all he was worth. A grunt was going to have to pass for a 'yes'.

"Mr. Sandoval, can you tell us what you witnessed this morning? Anything you remember would be very helpful."

Gus Sandoval put his fork down long enough enough to pick at a zit under his right nostril. Ripping off the head with a practiced, if grimy, fingernail, he eyed it before popping it into his mouth. He picked up the fork and resumed inhaling lemon meringue before he answered.

"I told Jack what I saw. White guy. Between five-ten and six feet. Weighed about a buck-seventy-five. Clean shaven. Military cut."

Ash sat gobsmacked and ashamed. Gus Sandoval enunciated each and every syllable, his text tight, his syntax precise. This homeless man, soiled and trembling, taught him a lesson worthy of a Harvard professor. He made a deal with god right then and there. If he could please keep Zoey safe, he'd stop being a pompous and judgemental dickhead.

"I wish I could tell you that he had three heads and cloven hooves that glowed in the dark. But, other than the dead body in his arms, he was just a normal guy. Being that I was on the far side of the bin, I didn't see his car. He pulled in and backed out. As you can imagine, my priority at the time was to remain undetected."

"We have a picture of the suspect, Mr. Sandoval. Did you happen to see which direction he came from, or in which direction he left?"

"I'm sorry. I wish I could be of more help, but that's all I know."

"You've been a great help, Mr. Sandoval. We'll be in touch."

Both he and Percy shook Gus Sandoval's hand, then turned to go. *Another fucking dead end.* Percy had one hand on the greasy door when he asked the owner one last question.

"By any chance, have you noticed a 'ninety-five Lincoln Continental with chrome spinner rims around?"

Jack pursed his lips to say 'no' when the guy playing cards with the cook jerked his head around.

"Ummm, I have..."

Chapter 41

The whore'll be out for hours...

Trapped in a nightmare of terror and torment, Zoey laid on her side and waited for death to ease her suffering. Yet, the human spirit is strong, and in some extreme cases, indomitable. When Billy Pickton left unexpectedly, a double jolt of adrenaline flooded her body and a tiny ray of hope penetrated her mind.

He's gone!

She didn't care why and she didn't care where. Her only concern was how long. Her entire body began to tingle. Whatever he'd shoved in her ass was starting to take effect. She couldn't allow that. Like she'd done for Billy Pickton, Zoey spread her butt-cheeks wide. Without a second thought, she extended her fore and middle fingers and dug deep. She could 'feel' the tablet in her bowels. If she couldn't reach and remove it, she'd have even less chance of survival than she did now.

Exploring the nooks and crannies of her anal cavity, her middle finger brushed against it. Zoey pulled her knees to her chin and scrunched her battered face. Pressing deeper still, she managed to curl the tip of one finger around it and guide it out. Relief swept over her, although she had no idea why. Considering her situation, it might have been smarter to leave it in and drift off into unconsciousness.

But...that wasn't her style...

Wriggling into a sitting position, she tried to clear her mind and get her bearings. The last thing she remembered was walking into a storage facility, hoping to find a phone.

What an idiot she'd been, thinking she was pulling one over on him when in fact, the opposite was true. Obviously, he'd led her there for a reason. It must be where he carried out his heinous crimes. Zoey winced, remembering the image of a dead and brutalized Gianna, her once sparkling eyes empty.

From her own eyes, tears welled and spilled. With her arms bound behind her, there was no way to dry them. Biting down on her emotions, she blinked them back. If she hoped to live long enough to scourge the abomination from her memory banks, she needed to focus. With that in mind, she tested the theory of looping her arms under her butt and around her legs. If she could get her hands in front of her, she might have a fighting chance.

Positioned as they were, she was as good as dead.

With all the strength she could muster, she pressed her fists into the spongy floor, bowed her elbows, and tried to 'walk' her rear end back through the opening. The position was ludicrous, even for an ex-gymnast. Twisting her body this way and that, she came close. But, close was light years from good enough. She collapsed, nearly breaking a crooked pinkie in the process.

The stress to her bad shoulder was excruciating.

Sweat poured from her naked body. Her breath was labored, barely eking its way past her pulverized throat. Still, there was little choice but to try again. Lifting her weight onto her fists, she dug her heels into the ground and tried to work up enough momentum to swing her hips through her arms. It was never going to happen. She needed an inch more clearance, if that. The idea that she was less than inch away from having the use of her hands drove her to the far edges of frustration and despair. It was just too close to contemplate.

How's your shoulder babygirl?

Like a phoenix from the ashes, Ash's words rose up from the depths of her misery.

Her shoulder! Of course!

Zoey knew what she needed to do. Sliding her right hand under the left, she took hold of the wrist. Sweat stung her eyes, her heart hammered in her ears. Taking deep, shuddering breaths, she pictured Ash's face and wrenched down and to the right in one sharp movement. Her shoulder separated from its socket, the pop as loud as a bullet. Waves of white hot pain tore through her, culminating in waves of nausea. Leaning over, she retched. Empty, her stomach produced only sour yellow bile. It sluiced its way up an already blistered windpipe.

Choking it back, it was time to try again. Any second, a sadistic lunatic might walk through that door. If this third time didn't work, she'd be out of ideas and sapped of strength. Her left arm hung at an angle, useless. Transferring most of her weight to the right, she hoisted herself onto her fists, using the left only for balance. Every muscle in her body convulsed from exertion. Like thread through the eye of a needle, her hips cleared her elbows with no room to spare. From there it was a simple matter of pulling her arms around and over her legs.

Jubilant beyond reason, she wasted no time in rolling into a squat and standing up. Agony radiated from her shoulder, her jaw, her eye. Even so, she couldn't pull the panties from around her throat fast enough. She used them to scrub the curdled ejaculate from between her breasts. Accomplishing that odious task, she dropped the undergarment as though it were contaminated with the

196

plague. And, in truth, it was: the black plague that was Billy Pickton.

Testing rickety legs, Zoey held her breath and inched towards where she believed the door was located. She was still a good eight feet away when she stepped on something cold and solid. Lifting her bare foot, she squinted down through the one eye that wasn't swollen shut. *Was she hallucinating, or was that a screwdriver?* Before it could vanish like a mirage in a sandstorm, she scooped it up. The eight-inch long screwdriver was a real as the plastic restraints binding her wrists.

Maneuvering the handle into the palm of her right hand, she crept towards the door feeling a trillion times more confident than she had just seconds before. Placing the screwdriver between her teeth, she located the doorknob. She turned it slowly, saying a prayer at the same time. When it didn't budge, hysteria took over. Double fisted, she used the screwdriver to stab at the door again and again, succeeding only in sending shock waves of agony to her shredded shoulder.

The fucking thing was sealed tighter than Fort Knox.

She whirled around, choking on panic. She'd come so far only to find that, indeed, she was inexorably trapped. There wasn't a window, wasn't a single chink in the impenetrable black armor. The human spirit may be indomitable, but, reality was impervious to such mundane cliches.

"AAASH..."

His name tore from her lips—half desperate plea, half poignant farewell. Throwing her head back, she looked towards the heavens and did the only thing left for her to do: she prayed. That's when she saw it. The spongy material in the far corner looked...buckled. It bulged outward, as if it weren't properly secured. One corner was torn, hanging free.

Past hope, she debated whether to just curl into a ball and go to sleep. The fact that it was right above the table piqued her interest. *Was it just a coincidence?* She hobbled over and peered up. There was nothing to see, but, there was even less to lose. With the screwdriver between her teeth, she braced against the table and climbed onto the folding chair. Her legs were the consistency of rubber, her traumatized brain was running on fumes. Undeterred, she stepped onto the table, which weebled dangerously under her weight. Setting her feet wide apart for stability, she reached up with bound wrists and tugged at the torn corner.

When the entire section fell open like a door, so did her mouth. In the drywall ceiling directly above her head was a metal access hatch...

Chapter 42

It was a simple enough contraption. A flat metal plate rested on a quarter inch lip about two feet square. All she needed to do was push it up and slide it back.

That's where the 'simple' ended, however. If her wrists weren't bound and her shoulder wasn't dislocated, it'd be nothing to scramble up into the rafters. A child could do it. But, her wrists *were* bound and her shoulder *was* dislocated. Considering that her life depended on getting through that opening, the predicament was untenable.

From the furthest recesses of her mind, years of gymnastics training flooded back to her. Her back straightened, her chin lifted. She knew girls that vaulted with sprained ankles, others that did bars with their palms ripped to the bone. Not only did adrenaline bestow the gift of super-human strength, it was also a natural anesthetic.

If she could just hang on long enough to swing a leg through, then maybe...

Just maybe...

There was no time to think about the damage she was about to do, nor the torment she was about to inflict. Clenching down on the screwdriver, she focused on the pain in her jaw and went for it. She caught the edge, knowing that if she didn't succeed on the first try, there wouldn't be a second. With most of her weight dangling from one arm, she employed strength, flexibility, and sheer desperation to swing a leg sideways, then up and over the lip of the opening. Transferring as much weight as possible to the leg, she hung motionless, gasping for air.

The next step was critical. Much like the Benton Twist, she would need to swing her other leg up, in, and across the first in one motion. At the same time, she would use that miniscule momentum to pull herself up, throw her good shoulder over the edge, and roll.

Sure...

She couldn't hang on much longer. It was now or never. Squeezing her eyes shut, she counted to three. An agonized scream filled her head, drowning out all cognizant thought. When she opened them to find herself face up between two ceiling joists, she had no recollection of going through the motions to get there. She was a wheezing, writhing, hundred and twenty pounds of emotional and physical wreckage. With her luck, she'd smash through the drywall and wind up back where she'd just escaped from. That unthinkable possibility was all the motivation she needed.

Carefully, very carefully, she pulled herself onto one of the six-inch high beams. Out of immediate danger, a wave of relief washed over her, dulling the physical pain. Every single muscle was in full-on spasm. Nonetheless, if she had to crawl naked on her belly across a bed of nails – or ceiling joists – she'd do so. Remembering her vow to Gianna and her love for Ash, she twisted around to pull the black padding back into place and slide the metal plate closed. Legs flailing, her foot kicked something.

Turning back, she saw it was an old shoe box. Her mind, stretched beyond capacity, didn't question its presence. If it were a flying monkey, she wouldn't have questioned its presence. Removing the screwdriver from between her teeth, she reached for it. The moment her fingers made contact, a tingle shot up her arms that had nothing to do with lack of circulation.

Ignoring her intuition, she lifted it onto her lap and removed the lid...

The faded picture on top nearly blew away what was left of her sanity. She remembered Billy asking her father to take it. They'd have made a beautiful couple, if only he weren't an up and coming psychopath intent on making her his first victim. As horrific as the photo was, it was the next one that had her gagging with revulsion. Recognizing a lifeless Jersey Stefanson, Zoey squeezed her eyes shut and looked away. She was all too well-acquainted with the gory details, thanks to the picture of Gianna she'd been forced to look at.

Sickened, she shoved the box from her lap. Dozens, if not hundreds of gruesome pictures spilled out. Her throat felt like someone poured kerosene down it. Every rasping breath was a match. She needed to get the fuck out of this nuthouse before she was nothing more than a grotesque photo in a lunatic's collection.

But...how?

The section of roof was about forty feet long and twenty feet wide. Overhead, a maze of rafters ran the length. At a gentle slope, she might be able to stand upright in the center. The 'floor' was a string of rotting wooden joists, one of which she was sitting on. They held up the ceiling in the torture chamber below. Two and a half feet of that thin, cracked, ceiling separated each one.

All of which was a boatload of useless information if there was no way out. It wouldn't take Billy Pickton long to figure out where she was. There was only one exit and it was deadbolted from the outside. For all she knew, he was already back. The thought made her weak in the knees and sick to her stomach.

Staying here was suicide by sociopath – guaranteed.

Zoey lifted her feet over the beam, turning to face the opposite direction. Peering down the forty foot length, she saw something that got her already racing heart beating triple time. Like the proverbial tunnel, there was a light at the end. Grabbing the screwdriver, she rose slowly to her feet. Balanced on the narrow joist, she squinted hard. On the far wall was an attic vent.

On the far wall was her only hope for escape.

From where she stood, it looked a galaxy away. In order to get there, her twitching, twerking body would need to traverse forty feet on a surface half the width of a balance beam. One wrong move could spell disaster. If she fell, she risked crashing through the expanse of unsupported drywall on either side.

There was only one solution. *She just wouldn't fall...*

Swallowing down her terror, she turned her feet outward from the hip and straightening her back. She hadn't the luxury of extending her arms for counterbalance. Slick from exertion and anxiety, she took the first tenuous steps towards freedom. Thanks to what she figured out was heavy-duty soundproofing, she couldn't hear anything that might be going on below her. She could, however, hear traffic from a far off highway and a train rumbling down its track.

She was halfway to her goal when she heard something that stopped her in her tracks. Squatting, she held onto the joist as she burst into tears. Not far off in the distance and closing fast were sirens. A shitload of them. For the first time, Zoey allowed herself to believe she might survive.

That's when the first bullet exploded through the drywall less than six feet behind her...

Chapter 43

Ash ground his teeth nearly to rubble. Every fiber of his being was saturated with a wicked concoction of adrenaline, hope, and terror. Percy had the pedal to the metal, but it wasn't good enough. He struggled to overcome the urge to jump out and run. In the thirty minutes since they'd left Billy Pickton's house, they'd gone from having nothing – to striking the mother lode.

Darryl Jenkins would never want for anything, Ash would see to that. The so-called 'manager' of the storage facility they were racing towards hadn't recognized Pickton's name, nor that of his alias. He was, however, able to describe 'Mr. Smith's' Lincoln Continental to a T, right down to the plate number. He'd also given them the master key, which he admitted he'd never once used in his twelve years of employment. He wasn't even sure it would work.

Mr. Smith had made a lot of revisions over the years...

Last but not least, Darryl Jenkins told them about a strange car that had sat on the front street for hours earlier in the day. It was there when he arrived – late – to work and it was still there when he left for the restaurant.

"Never seen it before. Some little furrin' number. Looked like a red and white coffin, ta my thinkin'. Just weird fer it ta be sittin' there, is all."

Like Mount St. Helens, Ash's head erupted from the intolerable pressure. *A red and white foreign number?* The Chief looked dumbstruck when he told him about the Fiat he'd seen driving at a snail's pace past the Waters' house, a large man hunched in the driver's seat. You could almost see his wheels spinning as he issued a second BOLO for the Fiat.

Squealing onto Petunia, their vehicle was one of about a dozen converging on the storage facility. The cacophony of sirens was deafening, yet, he was oblivious to it. His mind was laser-focused on one thing: finding Zoey alive. Anything after that they could deal with together.

I love you too...I love you too...

His sob was drowned out by the sirens. Seeing their destination looming before them, the sob contorted into a sustained and vicious growl. He wouldn't swear to not baring his teeth. Blocked from view by an eight-foot fence, only a faded sign and a row of shabby rooftops gave it away. Nobody knew if the son of a bitch was in there or not, but they were prepared for every contingency. Swat was right behind them.

As were the ambulances...

That's when the first shot rang out. It was followed by two more.

As Ash's bowels turned to water, two unmarked vehicle, four squad cars, and Swat peeled up the gravel driveway to the unit itself. The rest formed an impenetrable barrier on the street. Thanks to *Google Maps*, they'd seen the layout and knew this was the only entrance. The back end was just open field and railway tracks. They'd positioned a unit on either side of it, just in case. Percy pulled up to the curb, cut the engine, and turned to face him.

"This is as far as you come, Ash. If you can't give me your word, I'll handcuff you to the steering wheel. I'm not joking. What'll it be?"

Through his anguish, the blood in Ash's vein's was boiling. His hands were itching to wrap around Billy Pickton's throat and squeeze. If that son of a bitch hurt Zoey...

Percy reached for his handcuffs. Ash's gnashing teeth never parted.

"Fine. You have my fucking word. I won't come in."

* * * * *

Not thirty seconds later, he wanted to kill himself for making the promise. The cops had just started blathering into a megaphone for 'Mr. Waters' to come out with his hands spread and visible.

Fuck 'Mr. Waters' right up the ass!

Knowing the cocksucker was so close enraged him. It also scared the living shit out of him. What had he done to Zoey? Ash was sick at the thought. He couldn't just sit here – he needed to act. Before he could stop himself, he'd jerked the door handle and sprung from the car. With his hands clasped behind his back, he paced the sidewalk. While the cops and paramedics were fixated on the front entrance, he surreptitiously moved down the street in the opposite direction. Ducking between two houses, he jogged into the open field behind the storage units. The fence encircled the entire structure seamlessly. There was even less to see.

On the brink of a breakdown, Ash felt his heart crack in two. What little hope he'd had died with the first shot. Turning away, he was about to head back to the car when he heard it. It couldn't be, but it was. Barely a croak, the voice was that of a three-pack-a-day smoker.

"Ash! Ash! Oh my god! I'm up here!"

Just as he whipped back around, an attic vent came flying off its hinges and clattered to the ground. A figure he knew had to be Zoey stepped out onto a narrow 'porch'. His throat clogged at the sight of her, his legs turned to rubber. She was unrecognizable. For a split second, he once again envisioned his hands around Billy Pickton's throat. Unable to form words, rage and euphoria battled for supremacy.

Euphoria won by a landslide. Zoey *was alive!*

"Help me, Ash...please, please help me!"

From the corner of his eye, he saw a cop emerge from a squad car and start running towards him. His partner was on the radio, no doubt reporting the astounding turn of events. Ash didn't hesitate. Imbued with the strength of ten men, he faded back a few steps and charged. Never had an eight-foot barricade been scaled so effortlessly. His babygirl was less than ten feet above him. His throat muscles seemed paralyzed. There was so much he wanted to say but was forced to reduce it to three words.

"Jump, my love..."

Chapter 44

Zoey sat in the front pew, Ash on one side, Mama and Papa Ricci on the other. The church was standing room only, with the overflow spilling out onto the street. Seeing Gianna in a coffin was a harrowing ordeal, bordering on barbaric. The ill-fitting wig, garish make-up, and high-necked sweater did little to hide the surreal truth: Her best friend in the world was dead. She'd died a gruesome and violent death. She'd never see her, share secrets with her, or laugh with her again.

She'd managed to hold it together, but only for the sake of Gi's parents, both of whom were inconsolable.

It'd been three days since she'd leapt bound and naked into Ash's outstretched arms. Three days since he'd caught her pummeled body, dropping to one knee to absorb the impact.

"Marry me, babygirl."

She'd endured an unspeakable nightmare, but in Ash's strong, loving embrace, she knew she'd get through it. She knew something else, as well: she loved Ash Harrington with every cell, every molecule of her being. Looping her bound arms over his head and around his neck, she'd gazed into his eyes where his soul lay bared and vulnerable. It mattered not that one eye was swollen shut. She didn't need it to see where she belonged – and with whom.

She'd just enough time to nod yes before they were swarmed by police and bundled off to safety.

Since then, her life had been a swirl of doctors, shrinks, reporters, and police interviews. She found out what happened to Billy Pickton in the hospital, after emergency surgery to 'try' to repair her mangled shoulder. To say she didn't look her best was the mother of the mother of all understatements. A cross between a gargoyle and a mummy – her face was a black and blue fright, her arm was held in place with yards of white swaddling wrapped around her body. What little was left of her hair was 'styled' into what Peggy optimistically called a layered pixie.

With Peggy and Jock on one side of the bed and Ash on the other, Chief Percy O'Malley had stood at the foot, filling them in on the missing pieces.

"He tried to keep us at bay, kept screaming that he was holding a hostage. He actually expected us to stand down and let a serial killer drive off into the sunset."

The Chief paused to shake his head in disbelief. The smile he bestowed on Zoey twitched at the corners.

"Oh, yeah, I almost forgot. He promised to release you when he got to Mexico."

The mood lightened. Any granule of humor was welcome, even black.

"Although I hate to admit it, it was Ash that saved the day. Thank god the son of a bitch ignored my instructions."

Ash's guffaw caused her to giggle. Giggling hurt like hell, as did talking, moving, or breathing. The discomfort didn't stop her, though. On the contrary, it galvanized her. Zoey was floating on air, over the moon to be alive. The psychologist called it the Boomerang Effect. It happened after staring certain death in the face. The Chief's voice interrupted her meandering mind. Tuning back in, she hung on his every word.

"As soon as we got word that Zoey was safe, Swat rushed

the place. It was over in a matter of seconds. As we speak, he's over at Grace Memorial, under twenty-four hour guard. We thought it poetic justice that he got shot in the shoulder, but, quite frankly, I'd have been happier with a kill shot."

Ash seconded the motion before she had a chance to. Billy Pickton was a special breed of evil. As long as he was alive, he was dangerous.

Sitting on the hard pew, a chill went through her. Leaning into Ash, his arm came around her and held her close. The service was almost over. The thought of going to the cemetery made her stomach lurch. To distract herself, she looked down at the twinkling diamond on her left hand. She'd asked the nurse to cut away the bandages just enough to expose it. The thought of spending the rest of her life with the man of her dreams calmed her frazzled nerves.

In her purse, her phone was vibrating. Pressed close against Ash, she felt his go off at the same time. Frowning, she glanced up, but got caught up on the curve of his lips. When they mouthed the words 'you're beautiful', her unease was forgotten.

When both of their phones went off again, there was no distracting her. A kernel of foreboding took root in her heart, then raced through her veins like wildfire through tinder. For reasons unknown, terror gripped her. Something was wrong, she felt it. Using her one good arm, she worked her phone from her purse. Likewise, Ash pulled his from his pocket. As surreptitiously as possible, they swiped them open.

What she read had her doubled over in the pew. Her high-pitched keening filled the church, followed by Ash's anguished cry. Unaware of the pandemonium surrounding them, she held her phone so he could read it and he did the same. The messages were identical: They were to take shelter in place. Units had been dispatched to collect them.

Billy Pickton had strangled a guard and escaped from the hospital...

* * * * *

Epilogue

Three months later...

We, The People,
Gabriel Montero

Man's Body Found in Dumpster

Early Sunday morning, a man's naked body was found in a dumpster in Guadalajara, Mexico. He's been identified as Public Enemy Number One: William Waters, a.k.a. Billy Pickton.

Three months ago this accused serial killer evaded justice when he escaped from Grace Memorial Hospital, killing a guard in the process. According to authorities, Mr. Waters/Pickton did not die an easy death. Aside from being strangled, his reputedly underwhelming genitalia were nowhere to be found. Sources tell us a 'small' search is underway.

While We, The People would never condone violence, we celebrate the fact that sometimes – just sometimes – Karma comes around to kick the right person in the ass.

In related news, Ash and Zoey Harrington will be returning from their extended honeymoon at week's end. Rumor has it the couple is expecting. We, The People, offer a hearty congratulations and wish you both the best.

You certainly deserve it...

FALLEN

* * * * *

I hope **FALLEN** kept you **BALANCED** on the edge of your seat. If so, please do this Indie author the honor of leaving a short review. I appreciate each and every one. (https://www.amazon.com/dp/B01G4J1ZE0).

If you enjoyed this novel, please check out my other works:

MASTERED, Book 1, The MASTERED Saga
Erotic Romance, Dom/sub, Bondage, HEA
TRUSSED, Book 2, The MASTERED Saga
Erotic Romance/Adventure, Dom/sub, Bondage, HEA
The Naughty (And Naughtier) Adventures of ANGEL KNOTT
Erotic Fantasy, Bondage, Humor

About The Author

A sun worshipper, K.L. Silver lives in the frozen tundra of Central Canada. Perhaps that's why she writes HOT erotic romance, fantasy, and now, with **FALLEN** – thrillers.

Her children are grown and more importantly, independent. Her son has flown his Canadian coop and now resides in the state of Washington, where he works for Microsoft. Her daughter is a Red Seal chef. She awaits a grandchild with limited patience.

KL abuses yoga and caffeine in order to stay sane. Her first goal is to write great novels. Her second, of course, is world peace.

Namaste